The Ten Rules of Good Leadership: A Personal Journey of Discovery

Gavin Aspden

Dedication

To everyone who told me, "You should write a book about leadership,"—this is for you.

And to my wife, Hannah, whose quiet strength and constant support inspire me to be better every single day.

Acknowledgment

I'm deeply grateful to my father, who taught me far more than I ever realised at the time. And to my children—thank you for keeping me grounded and reminding me daily of the importance of humility.

I would like to extend special thanks to the exceptional leaders I've had the privilege of working with throughout my career. In particular: Marc Kerslake, Hywel Morris, Guy Tinsley, Gareth John, Simon Emery, Nick Brice, Amanda Line, Mark Protherough, David Hopley, Si Hussain, Jim O'Brien, Samar Sayegh, and Taimur Ali Mir. There are also several others whose names I'm not able to share, but their influence has been just as meaningful.

Finally, a massive thank you to my fellow partners and the incredible team I work alongside at PwC Academy in the Middle East. Your dedication, brilliance, and camaraderie make the work not only impactful but truly enjoyable.

About the Author

Gavin Aspden is far from the archetypal accountant or conventional 'Big Four' partner. His path to leadership has been anything but linear, shaped by a remarkable array of experiences that have given him both depth of character and breadth of insight.

In the vibrant chaos of the 1990s, Gavin began his professional life as a nightclub bouncer, later stepping into the brutal world of cage fighting before the sport gained mainstream recognition. His roles as a firearms-trained bodyguard and debt collector immersed him in the gritty undercurrents of society, while working security in some of the toughest neighborhoods taught him resilience, situational awareness, and the art of developing a thick skin. As a civilian contractor for the military and a front-row rugby player, he honed discipline, strategic thinking, and the value of cohesive teamwork.

Despite these high-octane beginnings, Gavin pursued academic excellence, earning a degree and qualifying as a chartered accountant. His transition into the corporate sphere as an auditor and manager was underpinned by a deep-seated passion for coaching and personal development. Whether mentoring elite athletes or guiding professional teams, his drive to support others has remained constant. His clients have included celebrities, politicians, and business leaders, and he is a sought-after public speaker and trainer. Based in the Middle East, he regularly fills conference venues across the region, where he now lives with his wife and three children.

Gavin's approach to leadership is rooted in lived experience. He embraces the philosophy that one either wins or learns. His finely tuned observational skills—refined through years in security and nightlife—have given him an acute understanding of human behavior, emotional intelligence, and communication. Whether in a boardroom, on the pitch, or in volatile high-stakes situations, he connects with people across all walks of life.

Fuelled by intellectual curiosity, Gavin has immersed himself in the disciplines of business, finance, strategy, psychology, leadership, and philosophy. He constantly applies theoretical frameworks to real-world scenarios, refining his approach through introspection, empirical testing, and an unwavering awareness of others' perspectives. This blend of street-smart pragmatism and academic rigor enables him to develop future leaders with clarity, empathy, and precision.

Having lived what many would consider multiple lifetimes in one, Gavin distills his experiences into a practical philosophy of leadership, captured in ten foundational rules. His journey is a compelling reminder that real leadership is not manufactured in a classroom but forged through hardship, humanity, and, as he would add, a well-timed dose of humor.

Table of Contents

Chapter 1
From Cage Fights to Boardrooms

Life goes in directions you never thought about. I would have laughed at your face if you had told me as a teenager, with raw, lacerated knuckles from working as an old school bouncer (or doorman as we called ourselves), that I would be a chartered accountant, partner at PwC in Dubai, and write a book about leadership. That was my world then – the nightclubs of the late 80s and early 90s, the thrill of a good fight, the adrenaline rush of pushing myself physically, and the camaraderie of people who shared my thirst for physical challenge.

The music was loud, the lights dim, and the air thick with testosterone and cigarette smoke. We lived for the surge. During those years, I always chose chaos over calm. But life happens exactly when you have other plans. My plan called for some brawling – at least initially.

And my early years were a testimony to that raw, wild energy of youth. I was a scrapper, always ready to prove myself in any dispute from the rugby pitch to the streets. It wasn't about winning so much as it was about refusing to back down, about showing that I belonged.

This innate desire to work myself physically, combined with a temper, propelled me into the gym, into amateur boxing, into multiple martial arts (but not really excelling in any of them), and eventually into the early days of cage fighting – the tough, no-nonsense sport that at the time was more chicken wire and warehouses than arenas and media. We fought in echoing spaces under flickering lights, sometimes on mats duct-taped to the floor, always surrounded by the unfiltered roars of a crowd that wanted blood, or at least the illusion of it. That metal clang, those grunts of exertion, the giving and receiving pain, and that 'crowd' roar were the sounds of my twenties and beyond. Pain was a constant companion, but so was pride. And beneath the violence was a strange kind of discipline—a code, even.

I never lost a fight in my cage fighting days because I never gave in. Whilst I can't say I never lost on the streets, I learned some hard lessons in the hardest of ways but still never stopped until I was stopped, one way or the other. Each battle tested my willpower – a battle against my own limitations. It was always about that one last punch. It was about digging down, finding that extra grit when my body cried out for respite, and showing myself that I could handle anything thrown at me. I remember nights when I walked into a broken fight, but something in me refused to bow and let weakness win. And this relentless drive – refusing to give in – would become my leadership style. It wasn't about commanding others with power but about inspiring through resilience. People don't follow because you shout the loudest—they follow because they see you won't fold, no matter the pressure.

That same energy found an outlet outside the cage in the sometimes chaotic world of nightclub security. Flashing lights, pulsating music, crowds of people trying to escape – an intoxicating environment that took a special skill set to navigate. There was a rhythm to it all, a current of tension and unpredictability running just beneath the surface. Being a doorman was more than muscle; it was about character. It was about reading people, understanding human interaction, and calming situations before they escalated into violence, but also not backing down when violence erupted. You had to be the calm in the storm, the unshakable presence in a place where chaos could break loose at any moment.

I learned to scan the crowd for troublemakers before they disturbed the harmony, those with amped masculinity who wouldn't spare a chance to create a show. I learned to de-escalate conflict with a calm disposition and firm voice, using words as my weapon. That meant knowing when to lean in, when to step back, and when to draw a hard line. Yes, sometimes physical intervention was necessary when others' safety depended on my ability to restrain an aggressor. Even so, I always used the minimum amount of force because I was protecting and not causing harm. There's a difference between control and cruelty—and I knew the line well. Behind the hard exterior was always the intention to shield, not to dominate. That was the code I lived by.

That night, guarding the entry to nightclubs was a crash course in human behavior. I witnessed the best and worst, celebration and rejection. I started recognizing the little things – body language and eyes – leading to confrontation. It was a valuable education in human interaction that would serve me well for years. Every smirk, twitch, or sidelong glance told a story. It was a frontline lesson in tension – how it builds, escalates, and sometimes explodes in seconds.

Even in the noise and chaos, patterns emerged. And if you paid attention, you could see the storm before it hit.

But behind the highs of the buzz around and late nights was something more motivating. Oddly, I saw myself as a helper, a bouncer. I was there so people could have a night out without being scared, so they could have fun. I felt like I was channeling my urge to fight to protect others. It wasn't just about standing at the door. Instead, it was about creating a space where people felt free to let go. I also did my part to improve other people's experiences by keeping the troublemakers out, by stopping fights. It was about defusing situations before they turned ugly, knowing when to step in with authority and when to hold back. That quiet responsibility gave me a deeper purpose, even if no one else noticed.

That urge to help – to make a difference – went beyond the nightclub doors. It took me to close protection, where the stakes and responsibility were higher. I worked everywhere as an armed bodyguard. The risks were real, and the consequences of failure were immediate. Lives depended on my alertness. The job required vigilance, quick thinking, and willingness to risk my life to protect others. It wasn't glamorous. It meant long hours, constant scanning, and a mental sharpness that had to be switched on every second. This role tested me physically and mentally and made me think about human nature and leadership. I began to understand that true leadership wasn't about control. It was about responsibility. About being the calm in someone else's storm.

Back then, I could see how those seemingly disparate experiences – cage fighter, bouncer, and bodyguard – were molding the leader I would become. They taught me discipline, resilience, and empathy. They taught me to read people, assess risk, and make split-second decisions under pressure.

They forced me to be both tough and tactful, to trust my instincts but also weigh the consequences. Mostly, though, they reinforced my faith in the power of helping others – a belief that would ultimately lead me to become a chartered accountant and beyond. Because in every role, what mattered most wasn't the title—it was the impact. And I knew, deep down, that helping others would always be at the core of everything I chose to do.

This Is Not a Hard Luck Story

So far, this reads like a rags-to-riches story, but it really isn't. I had advantages that others didn't have. A well-structured home discipline by my loving parents, who sacrificed things to provide for me, their only and adopted child. There is no doubt I was loved, but sparing the rod and spoiling the child was something, too, for those familiar with the phrase. They were firm but fair, balancing affection with expectations, always reminding me through actions more than words that love sometimes wears the face of discipline.

I was sent to a fee-paying school around twenty miles from home so I got used to early mornings and late nights from the age of seven. Those long commutes became a quiet training ground for resilience. I learned how to function while tired, how to manage my time, how to steel myself for a demanding day ahead before the sun had even risen fully. I could be a different person at school from who I was at home. I could study without fear of being bullied. I could work hard and pass exams. I was not a brilliant student, but I left school with a pocket full of 'O' and 'A' levels, which set the foundation for the more formal parts of my development and qualifications later on. My school was good but not brilliant, sport was encouraged and my love for intellectual as well as physical competition was developed young. I discovered early that strength wasn't only about muscle but about strategy and tenacity. That balancing academic work with physical activity brought a rhythm to my life, a way to release and recharge.

My school taught me many lessons. There were times when I was bullied by kids and teachers. There were times when I was encouraged, and there were times when I was made to feel stupid. Sometimes, these moments came within the same day. Nothing abnormal about my schooling. I loved it and hated it, as my own kids do today. It was a complicated, evolving relationship—school was both a sanctuary and a crucible. I am grateful for the sacrifices my parents made to send me there, and I am grateful for the foundations of my intellect that were developed there, but mostly for something that I was encouraged to have. Intellectual curiosity. A hunger that never quite goes away. I have always wanted to know how things work, what they do, where they come from and why, how much things cost, and why it is not different? This questioning—restless, persistent became my quiet companion through childhood, guiding me like an invisible compass toward places and ideas I would otherwise never have explored.

Trading Brawn for Balance Sheets

It certainly wasn't a straight, ascending line from nightclub doors to boardroom tables. It almost seems like a series of twists and turns of faith retrospective. But in the heart of everything was the drive to help others – to make a difference. That drive, though not always clearly defined, remained the compass even when the terrain felt chaotic or the destination unknown.

I found myself left in the world of close protection and doorwork but at a crossroads. Every pub was getting doormen, and the romance of being a nightclub doorman and the physicality of the job was becoming tedious; needles and knives were everywhere, and you could no longer rely on the gym gorilla standing next to you to have your back. The job had lost its shine; it had become more about risk than respect. Having dropped out of my first attempt at university life to focus on the more physical aspects of my personality, I decided, with the help of my first wife, to go back to university and get a degree. She saw something in me I hadn't yet fully recognized—a mind capable of more than brute force. She knew I had a thing to power through anything; it only needed some redirection. I had learned from the first attempt that submitting assignments and essays on time and doing the actual work was far more important than physical presence, and I ended up with a good degree from a great university, but it was still very much in the background to my life in the physical. My hands still carried the muscle memory of conflict while my head slowly began absorbing new disciplines.

But I found something missing. The adrenaline-fueled lifestyle was no longer appealing to me, and I wanted something new, something mentally almost as physically demanding. I no longer wanted ugly brawling outside nightclubs, but I needed something to challenge me. I'd always been interested in numbers, always had been a problem solver, and always had a certain order in chaos. There was something almost meditative in the structure of it all—the way columns aligned, how one figure fed another. So I took a shot at it – with a little self-confidence – and perhaps a little naiveté – and took the subject of my degree and got fully into accounting. It felt like stepping into an entirely different kind of arena, one where battles were fought with spreadsheets instead of fists and where precision mattered as much as presence.

I will not explore the details of late-night reading textbooks and accounting guidelines, answering exam questions, and studying properly for the first time ever. It was a learning curve, suffice to say. My earlier life had not truly prepared me for financial statements and audits. The leap from managing nightclub chaos to reconciling balance sheets was not an obvious one. But the determination that got me in the fighting cage also drove my academic pursuits and the politics of an office where headbutting someone was generally frowned upon! I embraced the challenge, immersing myself in debits, credits, balance sheets, income statements, substantive and compliance checking, and a whole load of other words that are somewhat depressing. Still, there was a quiet satisfaction in the discipline; it demanded an odd sense of control, maybe even redemption, in mastering the details that once seemed so far from my world.

It was a huge step to becoming a chartered accountant – a sign of my ability to adapt and learn. It led me into a world I couldn't have imagined – corporate finance, acquisitions and mergers, and strategic decision-making. And this was where I found a new application of my skill set. The rigorous technical foundation I'd built was now being tested in real-time scenarios where precision was important, and decisions could shift the direction of entire businesses.

I joined PwC, or Coopers and Lybrand as it was then because they're recognized for excellence and believe in developing leaders. It was a corporate environment compared with the nightclubs and back alleys of old. But the lessons I learned in those earlier years were relevant these days. The ability to read people, evaluate situations quickly, and remain calm under pressure were assets in high-stakes businesses. I realized that emotional intelligence, something rarely taught in textbooks, was just as critical as any financial model I might produce.

My first time with PwC was full of learning and growth. I developed analytical skills and an awareness of international business and financial markets. I worked with oil and gas, technology, and retail clients to help them resolve tough financial issues and reach their strategic objectives. Each client engagement brought its own personal challenge for me—tight deadlines, cross-border regulations, and challenging personalities—but these experiences sharpened my commercial instincts and helped me mature as a professional. It was the kind of adrenaline I was searching for.

I left after a secondment in South Africa and a return to the UK, a failed marriage and a lot of debt and stress from a close protection piece of work that went horribly wrong earlier and went into the professional education world. Back in the UK, I had found my calling. Drawing on my past and my present and helping others to pass the qualifications I had myself passed recently before. Progressing through the organisation to the director level and having had a succession of great mentors and leaders to follow. The shift from the front lines of finance to the classroom didn't feel like a step back. It felt like alignment. I found purpose in guiding others, simplifying complex topics, and witnessing when a struggling learner finally understood a difficult concept.

I then moved to the professional body that I belonged to with a large team, a big budget and an amazing boss and team around me. After 7 amazing years there, I was called upon to go back to PwC in the Middle East by an old friend and colleague, someone who has shaped my personality more than she probably knows and certainly taught me a lot about servant leadership. That call came at a time when I was ready for a new challenge, and it turned out to be a defining chapter. The opportunity to return, this time with more wisdom and experience under my belt, brought everything full circle.

This is now starting to sound like a CV or badly framed resume, so I would quickly pace forward to the key message of all of this. It is the people that made the experiences worthwhile and developed me. I was working with some of the greatest people in the industry, individuals who were experts in their area and also enthusiastic about developing other people. They weren't just technically brilliant — they were generous with their time, their insight, and their patience. I took advantage of that and learned from them — to take their knowledge and advice and contribute to the team's success. It wasn't just about absorbing information but about observing how they handled pressure, supported each other, and steered through situations with integrity and confidence. I had worked with some of the toughest and most resilient characters on the doors and in close protection. Some were currently serving ex-military, prison officers and police, teachers, tradesmen (and women). People from all walks of life, each carrying their own stories, scars, and skillsets. Some had been in prison, and many more probably should have been at some point. And yet, there was a code among them — a shared understanding built on loyalty, sharp instincts, and mutual respect. I have played rugby alongside the most amazing people who will drop everything to help a friend with a leaking water tank or broken-down car. There's a raw honesty in that kind of camaraderie: no questions asked, just action. Club rugby is not always the stereotypical public schoolboy scene. The club I played for in Bristol had people from every background but every one of them would go the extra mile for their mates. Plumbers, postmen, business owners, students — united by the pitch, the mud, and the unspoken commitment to have each other's backs. Everyone I have met in my life, the great and the terrible, the good and the bad, has contributed towards making me the person I am today. Every encounter has left a mark, some scars, some lessons, and some unforgettable friendships.

Ultimately, my second spell at PwC and my ultimate promotion to partner came from hard work, dedication, and a desire to help people. That desire was never performative — it came from a deep-rooted belief that when people are supported, they rise. My role is so diverse that even my wife can't explain it to friends when they ask. I lead teams, manage complex projects, develop thought leadership in the world of professional education, design upskilling solutions to enable individuals, organizations, and governments to achieve more than they think they can, and build personal relationships with clients. I wear many hats, sometimes all on the same day — mentor, strategist, problem-solver, and sounding board. And through everything I have done, I have never forgotten that underlying principle: helping others. It's the thread that ties everything together, whether it's delivering a keynote, drafting a proposal, or sitting down one-on-one with someone trying to figure out their next step.

And it was the desire to share these experiences and insights that sparked the book. Not to preach or to pretend I have all the answers, but to offer what I've learned in the hope that someone, somewhere, might find it useful — or at the very least, familiar.

Passing the Torch – Why This Book and Why Now?

It has been a turning point in my life to be a partner at a global firm like PwC. It resulted from years of successes and failures, determination and resilience, and a desire to learn and strive to be the best that I can be. I am not there yet, not by a long way, but with the help of the people around me every day, I get a small step closer. Each lesson, whether through triumph or setback, has layered itself into my foundation, shaping not just my career but my character. The journey has been anything but linear, and in its unpredictability, it has been deeply enriching.

It has been an exhilarating climb to where I am today. But, a year ago, my mother's dementia had deteriorated to where she needed 24-hour care. The deterioration continued, and she lost the battle in August 2024. As she died, it made me think about her memories and how I had watched them slowly fade over the cruel years of dementia. Her recollections of her life, the things she knew, and the experiences she had gone through were lost forever in the fog of the illness. I suddenly felt she had been selfish. I had learned so much from her, but it was a fraction of what she had to teach me. I was never a particularly good son, and we were never close, but strangely, I got angry that she had not taught me everything she knew. Now, I know that sounds odd, but I turned it into reflecting on myself. What happens if I lose my memories? I intend to continue in my journey of discovery about leadership, but maybe it is time to pause and reflect on giving back.

There's something profoundly humbling in realizing that a person can vanish even while still physically present and that their essence and wisdom can quietly slip away. The anger I felt was less about blame and more about loss: of untapped conversations, of quiet insights I never thought to ask for, and of time I thought I still had.

Perhaps a crash course on 53 years of learning from different aspects of life. The physical and the intellectual, from the doors to the boardroom, from the rugby pitch to the partner conference, from the streetfights to the presentations to global leaders in their fields and the occasional world leader. I feel that it is my responsibility to pass on what I learned. These aren't just memories but lessons etched in scars, in wins, in awkward silences, and courageous speeches. Not sharing them would feel like allowing valuable knowledge to go to waste.

I realized that my journey - as unconventional as it had been - provided me with insight for other aspiring leaders, regardless of their background or field. If even one person can bypass a mistake I made or accelerate through a hard-earned lesson of mine, then this sharing becomes more than narrative—it becomes purpose.

That is the reason I created the book. It's not about praising my accomplishments, name-checking, or showing off that I am a leadership expert. It is just about sharing my story - good, bad, and sometimes ugly - in the hope that it will touch another person and perhaps be useful to them in accelerating them through the learning that the life I have led has given me. I wanted to take off the armor, strip away the polish, and speak plainly because the real lessons lie in the unvarnished truth, not the highlight reel. It is about passing the torch of leadership to individuals who are following their very own leadership paths. And in doing so, maybe lighting their way just a little brighter, a little sooner, than I had mine.

The ten leadership principles I outline here are not taken from a few theoretical textbooks or academic research. They result from my experiences and from all the people I've met, worked with, and led along the way. They come from conversations in corridors, from watching others handle storms with grace, and from moments when I myself failed and had to get back up. These principles weren't crafted in a vacuum—they were lived, tested, challenged, and earned.

I wrote this book simply because I realize leadership can change lives and organizations. I know from experience how effective leadership can motivate people, produce high-performing teams, and create change. I've also seen the results of poor leadership: eroded trust, creativity stifled, and missed opportunities. I know what it is like when the alarm clock rings on a Monday morning, and you think, 'Yes, it's time to go to work,' and the times when you think, 'Oh sh*t, it's time to go to work' and how the leadership you experience or suffer can impact that Monday morning alarm clock feeling. That gut reaction—the one you get before your feet even hit the floor—often tells the story of the culture you're working in. It's a reflection of whether your potential is being nurtured or neglected, whether you feel safe or sidelined, whether you're energized or exhausted before the day even begins.

I believe everybody can be a leader, whatever the title or position. Leadership is about influence and not authority, job title, or hierarchy – it is about motivating others to take action and for them to want to take it because they believe in it and you. True leadership creates a ripple effect; it empowers others to lead in their own way, regardless of whether they're in the spotlight. It is about having a vision and providing others with the means and resources to make it come true. That means creating space for others to grow, to contribute meaningfully, and to feel valued not just for what they do but for who they are. Leadership, at its core, is deeply human.

My leadership principles are designed to guide effective leadership – principles that can be applied anywhere. These principles aren't prescriptive and rigid but may be modified and applied depending on the situation. Because no two teams, projects, or challenges are exactly the same, adaptability is essential. But if you apply these, or your, principles consistently then those around you know what to expect from you as a leader, and that is half of the battle won. Consistency builds trust. It creates an environment where people feel secure enough to take risks, offer ideas, and own their contributions without fear.

I want this book, more than anything, to be an encouragement and an inspiration. I want readers to picture themselves in my story – to identify their leadership potential – and to appreciate the rewards and challenges that come with it. Leadership is not without its tests. There will be times of doubt, failure, and discomfort. But if there's one thing I've learned, it's that those moments often hold the greatest lessons. When readers see themselves in these pages, I hope they feel both seen and equipped—to lead in ways that are authentic, courageous, and impactful.

I believe the world needs many more leaders who aren't scared of challenging the status quo, who serve others, and are driven to improve things. We need leaders who listen more than they speak, who seek understanding before offering solutions, who have experience before preaching, and who choose integrity even when it costs. And I hope this book can even help develop some of those leaders. If it helps just one person find their voice, step into their potential, and lead with intention, then it will have served its purpose.

Chapter 2
Personal Development of 10 Rules - The Compass Within

Leadership is an external process of compliance with policies and methodologies set down by your organisation from command and control structures to empathy and servant styles, fitting in models developed by corporate strategists and human resource specialists, which is great. However, true leadership is an extremely personal journey. It is about understanding yourself - your values and motives - and then applying that to guide and motivate others. It's not just about how you lead but why you choose to lead the way you do. There are thousands of books and tons of concepts about leadership, but the very best leaders are people who chart their own course using internal rules as their compass. These rules often bud from lived experience, moments of failure, breakthrough, and personal insight that leave a lasting imprint. Yes, you can draw on the experiences of others and their lessons learnt to develop your own internal compass. But it's in refining and applying those lessons to your unique context that real growth happens. And that is the intention of what follows. Before we get into my ten rules and start to develop your own, let's look at the principles behind them.

These are both generic and inflexible commandments. They assist you in defining your leadership philosophy, which includes key values and beliefs that govern your decisions and actions. They're not meant to be followed mindlessly, but to be embodied and adapted to the situations and people you face. Consider these ideas your personal code of conduct, guiding you through leadership and staying true to yourself. In moments of doubt, they help you find your center. In moments of challenge, they remind you of who you are and what you stand for.

Why are personal rules so essential to leadership? Here's why:

1. Clarity and Consistency:

It is easy to get caught up in competing demands, external pressures, and the changing tides of circumstance in the waters of leadership. Personal rules are an anchor – a firm foundation – which helps keep you focused. They bring order in chaos and help you make consistent decisions that reflect your vision and values without being overwhelmed by the situation.

They serve as an internal rulebook that cuts through noise and distraction, enabling you to respond rather than react. Without them, decisions become erratic, driven by urgency rather than purpose, and might lead to some regrettable choices.

Imagine a captain controlling a ship during a storm. Without clear rules, they would be tossed about by wind and waves without direction of where to head. However, with solid principles, they can confidently navigate the tempest, making adjustments as necessary while remaining true to their objective.

These guiding principles don't eliminate uncertainty but equip leaders to face it with steadiness. Personal rules function like a compass in moments of doubt, helping you stay aligned with what truly matters.

2. Building Trust and Respect:

Leadership is built on trust. You lead with integrity and consistency according to personal guidelines – you develop trust and respect with those you lead. People understand what to expect of you, they understand your values, and they know your actions speak for your words. This builds trust and is crucial for establishing relationships and a culture of collaboration.

Consistency in action builds emotional safety and gives space to openness and accountability. When those around you see a leader who doesn't bend their principles for convenience, they gain confidence in your decisions, even in difficult moments.

Think about a coach coaching a sports team. If the coach keeps changing his or her mind, playing favorites, or making decisions based on whims instead of principles or a strategy, the team will lose faith in his or her leadership. But a fair, consistent, and honest coach will win their player's trust and respect and build a unit that can do great things. That trust isn't given automatically—it's earned through a pattern of choices that reflect clarity of purpose. Over time, those patterns form the bedrock of high-performing teams and resilient cultures.

3. Empowerment and Growth:

Personal rules give direction to your own actions and help others learn and grow as well. By articulating your leadership philosophy, you provide all those you lead with a road map. They know your expectations and the values you place first and can act on that knowledge when making their own decisions and contributions. This creates ownership and accountability and encourages individuals to take initiative and achieve their full potential.

When people understand the “why” behind your leadership, they’re better equipped to align with it and extend it in your absence. Clear rules aren’t about control but about cultivating maturity, confidence, and independent thinking.

Think about a mentor guiding a young professional. By sharing their rules, the mentor offers a blueprint for success – principles the mentees could take and adapt to their own path. This allows the mentee the capability to make sound choices based on those principles, develop their very own style of leadership, and eventually succeed.

Leadership, then, becomes a multiplying force like a ripple effect. What begins as personal discipline grows into a legacy of empowerment that inspires others to lead with the same clarity and conviction.

4. Navigating Ethical Dilemmas:

Leadership is fraught with ethical quandaries. Personal rules can be your moral compass when making tough choices, even within organizational or professional body frameworks. They can point you toward choices that reflect your values and sense of integrity, often beyond simply compliance with the rules. They help you see the grey areas, resist temptations, and make choices you can confidently stand behind. In a world where rules often leave room for ambiguity, personal integrity becomes the differentiator between what you can do and what you should do.

Imagine an individual claiming a referral bonus for employing someone who had reached out to them through LinkedIn and was not part of their network. The rules might not strictly prevent it, but the principle of claiming it is wrong, as it was not referring someone that you thought was right for the role from your personal experience of working with them previously. It bypasses the spirit of the policy and turns it into a transactional loophole rather than a meaningful endorsement. The action may go unchallenged, but it undermines the very purpose of a referral system, which is rooted in trust and authentic professional relationships. Personal rules help you choose the path that best reflects your values. They serve as a private yardstick, often holding you to a higher standard than external expectations might demand.

My father always said about ethics, "Ethics drive what you do when nobody is watching, and you know you won't get caught." That kind of inner conscience doesn't just keep you out of trouble—it defines the kind of leader you are becoming.

Forging My Own Path

My ten rules for business success took its sweet time. Not a Pinterest-y weekend retreat with a whiteboard and a shelf of pompous self-help books was enough. It was messy and organic – from years of experience, setbacks, and successes. That process involved introspection, observation, and refinement based on the environments and people I've met.

Each lesson was earned, not taught and shaped by trial and error, not theory read from a book. There were no shortcuts to this road, just long days, tough calls, and the kind of learning you only get by being in the thick of it.

The Crucible of Experience

And those were very early years – far from the corporate world. The cage, the rugby pitches, and the nightclub doors were my training ground. They were tough environments that required determination, quick thinking, and a determination to succeed.
They sharpened instincts that no boardroom ever could – how to read a room in seconds, when to stand firm, and when to walk away. Each setting demanded presence, the ability to hold your ground when everything around you is in flux. It might not have taught me the rules of business, but it taught me a lot about human nature.

All these experiences were unrelated to business but taught me values that would be very useful in the corporate world. Discipline, perseverance, self-confidence, reading people, problem-solving, the importance of working with others, decision-making, risk spotting and management, and staying calm under pressure were the building blocks of my leadership style.

They became my unspoken toolkit that no textbook in a business school could teach you, and it was absorbed from lived reality. My challenges also taught me responsibility, adaptability, and the art of staying focused in chaos – qualities I carried to business. They made me comfortable with uncertainty and grounded under stress, which later proved invaluable when leading teams through high-stakes situations.

Observing Leaders – Good and Bad

I have seen many leaders along the way – from great mentors to weak leaders. I followed their ways of approaching things, decision-making styles, and interactions with others. What I learned was both the good and the bad – the qualities that built trust and respect and those that eroded morale and hindered progress. I watched how some cultivated loyalty without asking for it while others lost it without even noticing.

My best lesson was watching leaders who showed empathy and a willingness to accept that they did not have all the best ideas or solutions. They listened to everyone but were willing to make the decision and ensure it was implemented. Those people connected with their teams in a human way – they felt valued and understood and were contributing to the outcome and bought into the solution even if it was not entirely their own. They led from a place of strength, not ego, creating space for others to step up, and in doing so, they actually raised the whole team's performance.

I contrasted that with what I saw – where politics and self-interest, claiming credit and backstabbing others went ahead of integrity or transparency and how quickly that approach can break trust and undermine even the best teams. Toxic leadership spreads fast – it corrodes motivation and fosters fear, and soon enough, even the most capable people start holding back.

These observations determined what behaviors and principles I wanted to adopt and live by. They became a quiet compass I returned to often – especially in moments where the easier choice clashed with the right one.

Reflecting On Successes and Failures

Success is rarely a straight line. It's bumpy and paved with setbacks, challenges, and self-doubt. But through these experiences, we grow. I have always taken the time to reflect on my successes and failures, what worked, what didn't, and what I would change next time. Reflection has helped me refine my leadership style and personal rules. Without reflection, lessons fade and eventually become obsolete. With it, even failures become fuel. (Self-help books do teach you how to preach, though.)

When a project went well, I would ask myself: Did it really go as well as it could have? What made us successful? Was it luck, judgement, or heroics by individuals? Was it process or people? Repeatable or a one-off? I wanted to be sure we weren't just celebrating outcomes but also understanding the levers behind them.

I would go deeper when things didn't go as planned: How could I have improved? Did I delegate poorly? Am I judging something wrongly? The one rule I always had in debriefing when things didn't go well was to only use the word "I" and not "they" or "you."

It kept the mirror on me – not to shoulder all the blame, but to take ownership of the role I played and the influence I had.

These inner reflections helped me refine my approach not repeat the same mistakes and prevent blame. They helped me lead with clarity, humility, and a steady hand even when the path ahead was unclear.

Seeking Feedback and Mentorship

No leader can be alone. Everybody needs coaching and feedback. So, I've sought mentors and trusted colleagues who can give me constructive criticism and point out my blind spots. Their insights have helped me develop my leadership style and personal rules. It's easy to think you're self-aware until someone holds up a mirror you didn't know you needed. These conversations are sometimes uncomfortable but have often been the most transformative.

A particular mentor once challenged me to be more aware of my communication. He said my directness in some situations might be practical and effective in the moment but sometimes came across as abrasive. I had always seen honesty and clarity as strengths, but I came to understand that delivery matters just as much as intent. It inspired me to improve my communication, be more aware of my tone and delivery, and tailor my approach to different audiences. Not every situation requires the same level of force—some require precision, others patience. That little adjustment changed how I interacted with people, but there is always room for further improvement—especially with communication. It's a continuous process, one where self-awareness and humility go hand in hand.

My Ten Rules, Without Explanation

Here are my ten rules without any explanation. They can be interpreted in a number of different ways in different contexts and situations, and in the remaining chapters, I will try to explain what they mean to me and how they came about. These rules weren't born out of theory but emerged from trial, error, and experience. Each one has a story behind it, and together, they form the compass I try to live and lead by.

1. The answer is yes; what was the question?

2. Ask for forgiveness, not permission, and set your own filter.

3. All problems can be solved; it is the cost of the solution that varies.

4. Telling someone about an issue does not make it their issue.

5. Anyone can make a mistake; twice is stupidity, and three times is incompetence.

6. Do what you care about and care about what you do.

7. Everyone has an obligation to dissent if it is done appropriately and respectfully.

8. Being told when you have done something wrong is part of learning how to do it right.

9. A person's view is always based on the information they have. So, they are not wrong; they are just ill-informed

10. Earn trust and respect by demonstrating that you are true to yourself and your word.

Chapter 3
Rule 1: "The Answer is Yes, What Was the Question?"

Being positive and open can make all the difference in the world of business and leadership. The rule "If the answer is yes, then what was the question?" is about being proactive, collaborative, and solutions-driven. This is more than an optimistic catchphrase – it's a way of thinking that allows leaders to unlock potential, innovate, and build trust within teams and organizations. It challenges the default mode of hesitation and instead empowers people to explore what's possible, not just what's permissible.

A Foundation for Business Success

Opportunities don't always come packaged in glittery wrapping paper in the world of competitive and fast-moving businesses. They frequently take the form of challenges, requests, or ideas that initially appear out of reach or beyond capability. However, how a leader responds by saying "yes" sets the tone for how those situations unfold. A willingness to say "yes" reflects a growth mindset, one that sees potential even in the messy, the ambiguous, or the unfamiliar.

This is an important mindset because businesses need to be adaptable and agile at the same time. The business landscape is never static: competitors innovate, consumer behaviors shift, and external influences such as economic conditions call for fast reactions. Leaders who operate "yes-first" position their organizations to act proactively instead of defensively. In this way, they turn threats into opportunities and develop resilience to uncertainty. Being ahead of the curve starts with having the courage to move forward before all the variables are perfectly in place.

Saying "yes" does not mean accepting everything that is brought up blind-sightedly. Instead, it reflects a farsighted approach, a receptiveness to possibilities, opportunities, and solutions instead of hurdles. It's about changing the outlook from "Why this may or may not work" to "How can this work?" This small but profound shift of attitude creates an atmosphere where ideas can grow rather than be dismissed. Such a viewpoint encourages measured risk-taking, allowing leaders to look for newer, less obvious solutions. It’s a reframing that fuels creativity and encourages momentum rather than allowing paralysis to take hold.

For instance, if an employee suggests a new strategy for a project, a leader with a receptive stance will welcome it without any insecurity or pompousness. Even if the idea needs refining, the willingness to engage and collaborate boosts morale, showing employees that their contributions are valued and they are trusted. This underpins a culture of sharing ideas where team members feel more comfortable sharing ideas, resulting in better problem-solving and better results. When people believe their voice matters, they’re more likely to take initiative, challenge assumptions, and push boundaries in meaningful ways.

This proactive approach extends to interactions with external parties as well. Responding positively to requests from clients or partners develops relationships and goodwill.

For instance, agreeing to change timelines or customizing services shows you are committed to meeting stakeholder needs. Such actions might result in repeat business, referrals, and long-term partnerships, which might help the organization grow. A single "yes" can carry a ripple effect—cementing loyalty, enhancing reputation, and opening doors to future collaborations that may not have been visible at the outset.

Building Trust through Positivity

The nub for great leadership lies in trust. Employees, clients, and stakeholders will put their time, energy, and resources behind a reliable and supportive leader. Leaders need to nurture trust by saying 'yes' because it can't be brewed overnight. This rule demonstrates a willingness to find solutions, help team members, or resolve issues. It sets a tone that says, "I've got your back," and that sense of reliability becomes contagious within a team.

In terms of internal leadership, trust holds teams together. Team members feel respected and empowered when they see their leader prioritizing their needs and considering their input. That respect fosters accountability, not just loyalty. People step up when they know their voice matters. This trust is imperative for the organisation to grow and flourish with external partners. It shows the leader cares about far more than personal gain—he or she cares about the team or business success. And when people sense that, they work not just harder but smarter and more collaboratively.

When such an accommodating work environment is fostered, communication and transparency become more prominent. Leaders are open to ideas and feedback creating a safe place for honest conversations. Employees express concerns, share insights, and collaborate better when they think their leader values their point of view. This openness doesn't just increase productivity; it deepens connection and shared purpose. This dynamic is crucial during tough times like organisational change or crisis because, in a crisis situation, all the employees show ownership of the company and work days and nights to bring it out of the crisis. A trusted leader who says yes to worries and solutions reassures the team and motivates them to persevere through difficulties together. In moments of uncertainty, that kind of leadership doesn't just maintain momentum—it restores confidence.

Externally, trust built on positivity can set a business apart from the rest in the marketplace. Customers and clients appreciate organisations who are committed to their satisfaction. For instance, a company that doesn’t just dismiss complaints or special requests but acknowledges them keeps existing clients and enhances its reputation. It sends a clear signal: we care enough to listen, and we’re willing to act. Positive word-of-mouth from satisfied customers can amplify this effect and create new business opportunities. Over time, this becomes more than a strategy—it becomes a defining part of the company’s identity and strategically attracts unpaid publicity.

Encouraging a Growth Mindset

A leader who believes in the "yes" philosophy encourages the organisation to look at challenges as learning opportunities instead of obstacles to avoid. Saying yes to new ideas or tasks shows resilience and adaptability and the thrill to work. This behaviour reflects on their teams—encouraging employees to step outside their comfort zones and confidently accept change. It helps create an environment where experimentation is not only accepted but expected and where growth is measured by how often people choose courage over certainty.

Take, for instance, a business that must adopt a new technology. The transition may be daunting, but a leader who looks at it from the viewpoint of potential benefits can encourage his team to look forward. Saying "yes" to training, collaborative discussions, and troubleshooting demonstrates the leader is dedicated to tackling challenges together. That sense of shared ownership turns what could feel like a burden into a shared mission. This mentality gets ingrained in the organisational culture, and the business can adjust to a changing environment over time. Adaptability becomes second nature with time—not something forced, but something practiced.

You must also celebrate successes and learn from failures to encourage a growth mindset. Leaders who say yes to acknowledging achievements incentivize teams to do better. But they also acknowledge that mistakes are part of growth. They create a space where failure isn't punished, human errors are given space, and honest mistakes are not over-scrutinized—they're examined, learned from, and moved through. By transforming setbacks into learning opportunities, leaders eliminate the fear of failure and motivate employees to experiment and invent. Progress, after all, rarely comes without missteps along the way.

The benefits go beyond individual development—having a growth mindset. Organisations that follow this philosophy are better positioned to meet market demands and take advantage of emerging opportunities. Whether entering new markets, expanding product lines, or even becoming more sustainable—a "yes" attitude will help businesses stay ahead of the curve. It's a mindset that doesn't just survive change—it thrives in it and brings others along for the ride.

The Heart of Helping

And, it's also about helping people. If someone needs help, they may struggle to ask for it because of the fear of tarnishing their reputation. Being open and willing to extend a helping hand and support without needing to be convinced is important. Sometimes, the offer itself gives people the confidence they didn't know they needed. For me, my life has actually been about helping others. It took me many years to realise that helping was my motivation and some of the links are odd to think about in that way. Working on the doors was about helping people to enjoy themselves, rugby coaching, again, helping others. Bodyguarding—it's about keeping people safe and helping them achieve what they need to achieve. The job I do now, working as I do leading in a training business—quite an obvious one. When someone needs something, the answer is yes; what was the question? I don't need convincing or persuading. Helping is not just something I do; it's the through-line of my story. It connects every chapter of my life, even the ones I didn't recognise as service at the time.

The Ripple Effect of Positivity

The wider picture of this rule goes beyond the immediate results. When leaders say yes and act positively, they produce positive energy within the organisation, customers are more confident and motivated, and stakeholders have more faith in the business. This kind of optimism becomes contagious—it spreads across departments, influencing morale, performance, and the general atmosphere. This openness and collaboration define the organisation's top talent and build client loyalty. It sets a tone where people feel empowered to speak up, contribute ideas, and go the extra mile—not because they have to, but because they want to. It breaks that checklist mentality and fosters ownership.

Positive leaders also inspire their peers and their successors. They show that saying "yes" is invaluable and sets a high standard for leadership that values empathy, innovation, and collaboration. This kind of example sends a message—that real strength lies in enabling others, not controlling them. This legacy ensures the organisation's positive culture as leadership changes. It creates continuity, where new leaders step into a framework that expects and rewards optimism and forward-thinking.

Personal Anecdotes and Experiences

My "yes" rule has always been the foundation of my hustling and positive mindset. Saying "yes" has taken me places I never believed possible—that's the transformative power of that approach. It shifts the mindset from caution to curiosity, from fear to opportunity and accept everything heads on.

Doorman to Problem Solver

My time as a nightclub doorman taught me the power of "yes." While the job might appear simple—maintaining the peace and managing the flow of people—I quickly realized it was about much more than muscle and intimidation. It was about ensuring everybody inside was comfortable and safe. It meant reading situations before they escalated, using empathy before authority, and treating everyone with a baseline of respect yet firmly.

By saying yes to solving possible conflicts and helping somebody who needed assistance, I became a problem solver and a facilitator of good experiences. I learned that authority doesn't always come from being the loudest—it often comes from being the most present and willing to engage. This mindset has carried over to my leadership roles—I want my team to take ownership, resolve problems proactively, and contribute to an excellent work environment. I didn't want them to fear about mistakes but treat them as a chance. It's not just about reacting, but anticipating—and stepping up without being asked.

Training the Royal Marines

It was probably one of the most significant moments of my life when I was asked to teach the Royal Marines hand-to-hand combat. For a civilian instructor, that was a daunting proposition. Self-doubt crept in, and I could have said no because I lacked qualifications or experience. But something inside of me spurred me on to take the challenge. I said yes, and that word launched me into a bodyguard career globally. It was a turning point—one of those rare moments when saying yes didn't just change my path. It completely redirected it.

This experience taught me to push past self-imposed limits and look for opportunities to grow even when they seem out of our comfort zones. Confidence, I learned, isn't always something you start with—it's something you build by saying yes when it counts, like watering a little plant carefully enough to suffice it needs and provide it a space to grow. In the business world, this means being open to new challenges, taking chances, and believing that we can adjust and learn. Often, the skills we need reveal themselves once we commit—not before.

A Rugby Unexpected Love Story

The power of yes can affect our personal lives and our professional development. I hesitated to coach a female rugby team when asked to do it. I was not a rugby expert, and it seemed like lots of commitment. But I said yes, and that seemingly minor decision put me in touch with my future wife, the mother of our three kids. It's funny how life offers you the most meaningful rewards when you least expect them and often when you step into unfamiliar territory.

This experience shows us how life is interconnected and how opportunities can appear unexpectedly. What might seem irrelevant or inconvenient at the moment can shape your entire story in the long run. It serves as a reminder that saying yes to new experiences—even ones that aren't directly associated with our interests—may result in relationships, connections and life events we might never have expected. Sometimes, the most significant chapters of our lives begin with a simple nod to something unfamiliar.

Simple Ways to Save Lives

The most remarkable illustration of the power of yes was when I was asked to wash a celebrity car. It was a small job that I could have delegated and dismissed very easily. But by saying yes, I was where I had to be to prevent a kidnap attempt. It's surreal when you look back and realise how one decision, one small action, placed you exactly where you needed to be—not just for yourself, but for someone else.

This incident serves as a reminder that every opportunity—regardless of how small or trivial—can result in something worthwhile. There's no such thing as an insignificant task when it's met with intention and presence.

In the business world, this means valuing every interaction, every task, and everyone because even seemingly trivial contributions can make a big difference. You never know which small "yes" will lead to a life-altering outcome—for you or for someone else.

Lessons from These Experiences

These stories show how a "yes" attitude can change our lives. Accepting opportunities, going outside our comfort zones and facing challenges with a positive outlook opens a world of possibilities. It's not about recklessness—it's about recognising the potential in moments, even when they're wrapped in uncertainty. We produce growth, meaningful connections and a ripple effect of good that goes beyond us. The impact of that mindset isn't just personal but cultural, organizational, even generational.

This philosophy has shaped how I lead—to promote collaboration, empowerment and proactive problem-solving. It reminds us that saying "yes" means more than taking on tasks or even finishing requests—it means accepting a state of possibility where challenges are regarded as opportunities and every interaction as a chance for growth and change. In a world often governed by hesitation, "yes" remains a quiet act of courage—one that multiplies in ways we can't always predict but will always feel.

Practical Applications in Business

Though simple in concept, saying "yes" requires considering its practical application in the nuanced business world. This is not about rushing into every request or undertaking every challenge blindly. It all comes down to developing an attitude of opportunity, collaboration, and positive action. A "yes" mindset doesn't mean abandoning discernment; it means choosing engagement over resistance where growth is possible.

Some examples and strategies for using the "yes" rule in your everyday business interactions:

1. Start with Small "Yeses"

Start small if you're not accustomed to a yes mentality. Say yes to helping a colleague with a task outside your normal responsibilities. Say yes to networking—even if you feel introverted. Say yes to tackling a little project that tests your limits. These small "yeses" will build momentum and confidence for bigger opportunities. They act as stepping stones, conditioning you to respond to uncertainty with curiosity rather than hesitation.

Example: A colleague demands that you proofread a presentation—which is not your job. Say yes instead of berating them. That little help builds goodwill and strengthens your working relationship. It signals that you're someone who contributes beyond your title, someone others can trust in a pinch.

2. Reframe Challenges as Opportunities

In case you are facing a challenge and want to default to "no," rather than saying "no," ask yourself: "Why do you default to 'no'?" What if I said yes? Reframe the challenge as a learning opportunity or innovation opportunity. This perspective shift may unlock unexpected solutions. Often, we reject challenges not because of their complexity but because of fear—of failure, judgment, or discomfort.

Example: You have a project that seems overwhelming to your team. Instead of focusing on obstacles, say yes to the challenge. Brainstorm ideas for solutions, tap into your team's strengths, and see the project as an opportunity to prove yourself. Difficult situations often reveal undiscovered capabilities—both in yourself and those around you.

3. Be a "Yes, And..." Person

In impromptu comedy, this "yes, and..." principle encourages participants to accept and build upon offers. Use this in your business interactions. Say yes, and when somebody brings up an idea, rather than saying no, say "yes, and..." and add your ideas or suggestions. This helps with collaboration, creativity, and a more positive work environment! It shows you're not just there to speak your mind but open enough to engage with their thinking and enriching it.

Example: Team member suggests a new marketing strategy. Say yes, and add your thoughts or suggestions on improving it instead of dismissing it completely. You might find that their idea—when combined with your perspective—sparks something neither of you would have conceived alone.

4. Set Boundaries and Prioritize

A "yes" mentality can be helpful, but you must define boundaries and prioritize commitments. Not everything you can say "yes" to. Seek out what opportunities match your goals, values, and capacity. Say no to requests that drain you or distract you. Saying yes to everything blindly dilutes your energy and diminishes the impact of your efforts.

Example: Your plate is full of work—now a colleague asks you to take on another one. Saying no here means you're at capacity but would still like to help in the future. A clear, respectful "no" preserves your bandwidth and maintains relationships without compromising your responsibilities.

5. Cultivate a Culture of Yes

You can lead by creating a "yes" culture in your team or organization. Encourage proactive problem-solving, reward initiative, and celebrate successes. Make people comfortable taking chances, sharing ideas and facing new challenges. When people believe their input matters, they're more likely to take ownership and push boundaries in a healthy, productive way.

Example: Establish a suggestion box for employee input on improvements. Honour those who contribute innovative solutions. Create a culture where yes is the default response to new ideas and initiatives. This simple shift can transform passive employees into engaged contributors.

6. Communicate Effectively

Clarity in communication is key to implementing the "yes" rule. Say yes to a request if you understand the task, have realistic expectations, and mention limitations or concerns. This helps everyone stay on the same page and prevents miscommunications or disappointments! Being agreeable does not mean being vague—it means being responsibly transparent.

Example: A client asks you to finish a project by a deadline. Say yes, but spell out challenges or resource limitations. This helps manage expectations and avoid conflict later. It shows professionalism and builds trust, as you're upfront about potential constraints while still showing commitment.

7. Embrace Continuous Learning

A yes mentality often means going beyond your comfort zone and taking on new challenges. Accept this as a learning experience. Look for training, mentorship or resources to learn more. Every "yes" can be a doorway to a skill you didn't know you needed and eventually capable of mastering.

Example: Now, you lead a project using a new technology or methodology. Say yes—learn about new tools or techniques. This increases your skill set and makes you an invaluable asset to your team. More importantly, it positions you as someone who evolves with the landscape rather than resists it.

Applying such concrete steps will help you create a "yes" mindset in your business dealings, in collaboration, and in creating new chances for growth and success. Remember that it isn't all about saying yes. Rather, it's about having an attitude of possibility—that challenges are opportunities and every interaction can be a change agent. It’s a mindset shift, not a surrender of discernment. When applied thoughtfully, saying "yes" becomes a strategy, not just a response.

Chapter 4
Rule 2: "Ask for Forgiveness, Not Permission, and Set your own Filter."

The Power of Initiative

So ask for forgiveness and not permission - the rule might seem rebellious initially, but it represents a fundamental principle that has shaped who I am all my life: To ask for forgiveness and not permission. The importance of initiative. It is about standing behind your convictions, trusting your judgment, and controlling your choices - whether you know it will work or you will get some things wrong. This rule encourages bold action and has taught me that taking initiative, even in uncertain situations, is often the spark that leads to progress.

Taking the initiative involves more than completing tasks or following instructions passively. It means searching for ways to contribute, resolve issues before they worsen, and make a difference in your staff and business. It is about stepping up and assuming responsibility for going ahead instead of waiting for somebody else to give you direction or permission to act. I've learned through personal experience that the best breakthroughs often come from simply choosing to act when others hesitate.

This proactive attitude is essential for good leadership. Those with initiative inspire their teams to have a positive attitude and to go the extra mile. They build momentum by identifying opportunities and taking action rather than awaiting things to happen. They instigate innovation by trying new ideas and approaches, sometimes even challenging the status quo. They don't run from challenges or get wrapped up in chasing approval at every opportunity. Instead, they go with their gut, make sound decisions, and take calculated risks to get there. While this mindset can feel risky, you can mitigate potential setbacks by preparing well and reflecting on the consequences before acting.

However, taking the initiative is only one side of the coin. That should balance with a sense of accountability. You also assume all the risk when you act of your own will- bad or good. This includes recognizing mistakes, gaining knowledge, and making amends if needed. And it means listening to feedback - knowing that even good intentions can have unintended consequences. Being accountable means facing the results of your actions head-on, whether those results confirm your decision or expose areas for growth.

And accountability does not involve blaming or punishing. It's about owning your decisions and outcomes and showing commitment to learning and growth. It means being truthful with your team if things do not go as planned. This builds trust and respect - you show your team that you admit to making mistakes and are committed to improvement. When I've admitted missteps in the past, I've seen how it fosters a culture where others also feel safe to take initiative, knowing they won't be shamed for honest errors.

Initiation coupled with accountability creates a powerful dynamic within people and teams. That enables people to act confidently, and they can choose and own what they do. This creates trust, respect, and collaboration, where people feel they can contribute their best and own their successes and failures. In my experience, this balance between action and responsibility not only drives results but also creates a workplace where people thrive and grow together.

The filter approach and setting your own.

I believe that everyone should set their own filter for those around them. No matter whether you are the most junior or senior member of the team, you should have a filter for tasks. Taking the initiative starts with how you filter priorities—owning your actions and understanding the boundaries within which you can lead.

Let's say you are faced with ten tasks. Tasks one to three are things you should just do, don't tell anyone about, and just get on with them. For tasks four to six, you do and let your boss know you've done them as they should be aware. Seven through nine are things where you identify a proposed solution with alternatives, present them and get support for your decision because they might involve others or expose the organization to risks that are beyond your level. Item ten. This is the big red panic button, the issue that you look at and need help to come up with an answer or way of solving the problem. This kind of tiered decision-making allows space for initiative while also respecting the chain of accountability—key when living by the rule of asking for forgiveness, not permission.

Your team should set their filters with you, and you should set yours with your bosses. Part of teamwork is setting the filters at the right level for each other. Without clearly defined filters, team members can hesitate to take action, especially when they're unsure about the risks—this is where thoughtful initiative becomes critical.

Ask for forgiveness, not permission - that is the call to action for proactive leadership. It serves as a reminder that we all can easily make a positive change, change things, and decide our destiny. It's about accepting that power and acting with conviction and conviction.

This has been my rule all my life - taking measured chances, tackling challenges, and making choices that shaped my life and career. Several examples from my own experiences show how taking initiative and being accountable for your actions have helped me achieve success and learning experiences. Of course, it’s not a risk-free path—missteps happen, but taking ownership of outcomes is part of what makes this mindset so powerful and respected.

Success Stories

Ask for forgiveness, not permission, has been my constant companion. It's brought some of my best successes - showing initiative and accountability in action. Here are a few stories to illustrate this principle in practice. These examples show how thinking independently and stepping forward in moments of uncertainty can unlock opportunities others might miss.

The Unconventional Approach:

I once guarded a very high-profile CEO at a conference in a politically unstable region. The usual security protocol called for a bodyguard team, armored vehicles, and a planned route with options for variation. However, I checked the situation and saw several possible holes in the plan. The route ran through an area notorious for challenges in the past, and we might be a more visible target with the armored vehicles. I knew this was one of those moments where hesitation could be costly—initiative had to take precedence over protocol.

I proposed an alternative security strategy instead of following the established protocol. I suggested a less conspicuous approach, utilizing a network of local contacts to gather intelligence and navigate the city discreetly.

My suggestions initially got resistance. Some questioned my authority over going outside the standard protocol, and some were alarmed by my perceived risk-taking. But I persisted, confidently explaining my rationale and the potential benefits of tackling security more proactively and adaptively. Navigating these objections was part of the risk—one that can be mitigated through strong communication, preparation, and confidence in your reasoning.

Ultimately, my initiative got approved, and the revised security plan worked. The CEO made it through the conference safely, and my proactive approach earned the respect and trust of colleagues and clients. This experience reinforced my belief that initiative can create positive outcomes even when initially resisted. The decoy vehicles were stopped on the original route at a ‘checkpoint’ put in place by local militia that morning. This outcome proved the power of trusting your instincts and stepping up, even in high-stakes environments.

Friendship and trust in others:

In another instance, I had a friend who was having a crisis financially. He had difficulty raising money to save his entrepreneurial venture as he had hit a plateau. Existing investors and lenders were wary of adding to the pile. He asked me to inject some money initially but I said I would, only if he let me look at the business properly.

I started looking at both his personal and business finances, considering a combination of other financing options, such as government grants, private equity investment, and strategic partnerships. I also helped him with pricing and market penetration. And a bit of cash.

My approach to the problem of a friend taught me a lot about trust. It was a hobby business for him, a retirement plan perhaps. However, he had doubled down and stood to lose quite a lot of it failed. His trust in me as a friend meant a lot to me, and that level of trust is rare. This situation also called for the principle: 'Ask for forgiveness, not permission.' I didn't wait for an official invitation—I acted with care, trusted my instincts, and took the initiative to help where I knew I could.

Lessons Learned:

These stories and many others over my career have reinforced the value of initiative. Acting on my convictions, trusting my judgment, and owning my decisions have helped me achieve results, build relationships, and contribute to my teams and organizations. Many times, when I acted before receiving formal approval, the outcomes were surprisingly positive—especially when my motives were genuine and solutions-oriented.

Of course, taking the initiative comes with its risks. Occasionally, your actions do not work out, or your decisions are opposed or criticized. But then again, admitting to your mistakes is a great leadership quality. When asking for forgiveness instead of permission, it's important to remain accountable and open to criticism—that's how you grow and earn continued trust.

The challenges this approach may pose and ways to mitigate those risks while retaining initiative are discussed next.

Navigating the Risks of Initiative

While taking the initiative has power, it also comes with risk and challenge - "Asking for forgiveness, not permission" requires discernment, a strong ethical guide, and willingness to make mistakes. The essence of this rule lies not in recklessness but in acting when the timing is critical—balancing courage with conscience. I've faced situations where I jumped into action too quickly and later realized I had crossed a line unintentionally, but those moments taught me more about how to weigh context with urgency.

Some of the potential pitfalls and strategies for mitigating those risks:

1. Overstepping Boundaries:

The biggest risk with initiating is that you may overstep your boundaries - whether your role, organization culture, or colleagues' or superiors 'expectations. Acting without context or repercussions can have unexpected results - damaged relationships - even disciplinary action.

Mitigation Strategies:

Develop good communication skills: communicate your intentions and reasoning before acting - especially if your initiative involves areas outside your control. Seek feedback and input from others to ensure your actions match the team's goals and your organization's values.

Know your responsibilities and role: Know your role in the organization and your authority. Avoiding activities outside your expertise and responsibility can be proactive - but not without seeking advice or approval.

Respect the chain of command: initiative is great, but so is respecting your organization's established hierarchy and decision-making. If your initiative involves higher-up approval, follow the right channels and procedures. Taking the initiative within the rule of 'asking for forgiveness' still demands tact—respecting boundaries while recognizing when bold action is needed.

2. Creating Unnecessary Risk:

Sometimes, taking the initiative involves taking a risk. However, you must differentiate between calculated risks supporting your organization and reckless actions that could undermine its success. Impulsively acting without considering the consequences can cause costly mistakes, damaged reputations, and missed opportunities. I remember making a fast decision on a team project—fortunately, it paid off, but it highlighted how vital it is to pause briefly, assess risks, and then move.

Mitigation Strategies:

Learn risk assessment skills. Before you act - weigh the benefits and risks of your initiative. Consider the impact on your team organization or stakeholders. If the risks outweigh the benefits, you may want to rethink your approach or get additional guidance.

Seek diverse perspectives: Don't rely solely on your judgment when assessing risk. Consult colleagues, mentors, and experts for additional perspectives and insights. This may reveal potential blind spots and help you make better decisions.

Plan for the unexpected: Even the best-laid plans can go sour. Consider challenges or setbacks before you take action and make a contingency plan for them. This will limit risk and the impact of unexpected events. 'Ask for forgiveness, not permission' should never be mistaken for recklessness—proper planning can make bold moves successful, not chaotic.

3. Alienating Colleagues:

Taking the initiative may seem like stepping on toes or taking credit for someone else's work. You risk resenting coworkers and creating a hostile atmosphere if you do not seem supportive or cooperative. I've learned that strong initiative must be tempered with humility—taking action should never feel like claiming territory.

Mitigation Strategies:

Foster a collaborative approach: your initiatives should focus on teamwork and collaboration. Seek input from colleagues, acknowledge contributions, and credit for successes. This creates trust and ownership.

Communicate effectively - state your intentions and justification for taking the initiative. Outline how your actions will benefit your team and organization. Be transparent about your decision process and open to feedback.

Be mindful of your communication: Be assertive but not dismissive of ideas offered by others. Listen actively, respect other perspectives, and be open to compromise. Even when you move first, making space for others builds loyalty and shared purpose—turning individual initiative into team success.

4. Burning Out:

Sometimes, taking initiative means going beyond your normal duties. Although this is rewarding, you must also know your limits and avoid taking on more than you can handle. Overextending yourself can cause burnout, stress, and lower productivity. I once learned the hard way that doing more doesn't always mean doing better—it's essential to pick your moments and preserve your energy.

Mitigation Strategies:

Prioritize your commitment: Not all initiatives are equal. Learn to prioritize commitments based on importance, urgency, and goal alignment. Say no to requests that drain you or distract you.

Do self-care: initiative takes energy and focus. Take proper care of yourself emotionally and physically. Sleep enough, eat right, move around regularly, and take breaks as needed.

Try to delegate effectively - Don't try to do it all yourself. When appropriate, delegate tasks to others and let them share the load. Following the rule of 'ask for forgiveness' doesn't mean you carry the world on your shoulders—it means you act boldly but also wisely.

5. Not Learning from Mistakes:

Taking the initiative inevitably involves making mistakes. However, the true value of this method is learning from all those mistakes and enhancing your decision-making. If you do not admit your mistakes or resist constructive feedback, you miss out on growth opportunities. I've found that reflection after bold action is where the real magic lies—when I've misstepped, owning it quickly helped rebuild trust and refine my leadership.

Mitigation Strategies:

Embrace a growth mindset: View mistakes as learning opportunities, not personal failures. Analyze what went well, where you can improve, and learn from it for future initiatives.

Seek feedback actively - Don't wait for feedback. Actively seek constructive criticism from colleagues, mentors, and superiors. Be open to other perspectives and willing to adjust how you approach things.

Create a culture of psycho-safety: Let people take risks and admit mistakes without fear of retribution. This encourages learning and invention, allowing your team to succeed. 'Ask for forgiveness, not permission' works best in an environment that values resilience, transparency, and reflection over perfection.

Chapter 5
Rule 3: "All Problems Can Be Solved; It Is the Cost of the Solution That Varies"

The Leader as Problem-Solver

Leadership is about steering through problems and finding solutions. Whether you're leading a team or a company or perhaps simply yourself, the capability to recognize, analyze, and solve problems is crucial for success. It's what separates someone who merely manages from someone who leads. Firefighting is more than putting out fires. Proactively looking for opportunities to improve and anticipating challenges means leading your team to a better future. It requires foresight, discipline, and the courage to lean into discomfort before it erupts into chaos.

Problems are inevitable when you are in a business. These can have an internal cause—communication breakdowns, process inefficiencies, or conflicting team priorities. Or they can also be caused by external influences like market movements, regulatory changes, or unexpected crises that interrupt normal operations. What matters most is not the origin of the problem but the response it receives. Leaders who take ownership early can steer the course before things spiral.

Good leaders face the problems rather than getting dejected. They see them as chances for development and innovation. The acquirers have a mindset that challenges are puzzles to be solved, situations to be navigated, and opportunities to grow and improve. And they understand that even the most daunting problem can have a solution, and while looking for it, can often produce valuable insights, stronger teams, and more resilient organizations. You don't know what you are capable of until you're put to the test. In this sense, problems aren't obstacles but an invitation to evolve.

I feel really pumped when someone says something is not possible. I have never faced something that is genuinely impossible. Usually, it is under-resourced, there is no budget, or there is no time. Almost always, resources can be found, cash can be paid, or deadlines can be moved through communication, so a solution can be found. What we often label as "impossible" is simply "inconvenient" or "impractical" at that moment. But both time and perspective can shift those limitations. The biggest enemy to this, I find, is when everyone starts having an armpit fire…

When things get challenging, many people act like their armpits are on fire, running around, creating havoc, and flapping their arms around—like if their armpits were on fire. This is massively counterproductive. Leaders are calm in crisis. Leaders inspire those around them to also be calm. That composure is contagious. It sends a silent but powerful message: we've got this.

So why is problem-solving so important for leaders? Here's why:

1. Building Trust and Confidence:

Demonstrating that leaders can solve problems builds trust and confidence in teams and stakeholders. You see, behaviours and gestures are contagious and passes on to people. People feel safe that their leader can meet challenges, make sound decisions under pressure, and lead them to solutions. This gives a feeling of security and stability, even in times of uncertainty, that the team can overcome anything with their leader leading. When a leader remains composed, applies structure to chaos, and still moves forward, it reassures everyone that the situation is manageable, even if it isn't yet resolved.

2. Driving Innovation and Progress:

Problem-solving drives innovation and progress. Leaders who identify challenges and respond effectively pave the path for a linear improvement. They challenge their teams to think critically about assumptions, new ideas, and creative solutions that go beyond the bounds of what can be done. Instead of seeing limitations, they encourage a mindset that asks: "What if?" or "How might we?" This creates a fluid and flexible environment wherein progress is made and the organization is ever evolving to meet new opportunities and challenges. A culture of innovation thrives where leaders reward initiative and welcome complexity, not avoid it.

3. Enhancing Decision-Making:

Problem-solving is related to decision-making. Leaders who analyze situations thoroughly, find root causes and evaluate possible solutions are better positioned to make sound decisions that produce positive outcomes. They do not go by gut feeling or make hasty decisions. They process information and perspectives carefully before making a decision. This rigor in thought process filters out emotional reactions, replacing them with structured reasoning and clarity. This gives them credibility and makes them a stronger leader because their team knows they can make sound judgments for the organization in general! Over time, that consistency becomes part of the leader's reputation—a steady hand in both calm and storm.

4. Fostering Resilience

Not denying it, setbacks and challenges are part of leadership. Leaders who can solve problems better are resilient to hardship. They see obstacles as chances to learn and grow, not barriers to success. Each difficulty becomes a test of adaptability, not a marker of defeat. They don't give up easily or become discouraged by setbacks; they never give up hope. Instead, they evaluate the situation, learn from it, and modify their approach accordingly. They operate from a belief that solutions are always possible, even if not immediately apparent. This resilience motivates their teams to tackle tough situations with confidence that their leader will weather the storm. When people see a leader stand firm during turbulence, they are more likely to hold their own ground as well.

5. Creating a Positive Impact

Good problem-solving ultimately leads to change. Those leaders who can meet challenges effectively create a positive ripple effect in their teams, organizations, and society. They become agents of progress, not just crisis managers. They get people moving, helping them find solutions, and just like that, they change the world. This doesn’t always mean dramatic transformations; sometimes it’s in the quiet course corrections that steer things back on track. When they confront issues directly, they show a desire for improvement, innovate, and aim for a better future for all. They don’t just fix what’s broken—they build something stronger in its place.

Mastering the Art of Problem-Solving

Problem-solving is critical for any leader, but you do not acquire it naturally. The process can be learned and refined with practice and experience. It's a skill that’s honed through both success and failure, through trial and reflection. Below are some strategies I've found to be most useful in my own journey:

1. Identify the Real Problem

You need to know what you are dealing with before you can solve it. It’s like knowing your enemy before putting up a fight. This is probably obvious, but people fall down. Be precise about the problem, its scope, and possible impact. Don’t chase symptoms—search for the root. Ask yourself:

What symptoms does the problem have?

Exactly where and when does this problem occur?

Who is impacted by the problem?

What are the consequences if that issue isn't fixed?

Example: A company notices a significant drop in sales and suspects that it was due to aggressive pricing by the competition. The plan was to offer deep discounts and a new marketing campaign focusing on the discounted price. After conducting further analysis, the stores department identified an increase in returns due to quality issues, which was traced back to a new supplier. The market had responded due to influencer comments.

The problem to be solved is the quality issue, and then to focus on a marketing approach based on quality, and perhaps not so much on price. It's a classic case of diagnosing beyond the surface. Misidentifying the issue would have meant spending money in the wrong places and worsening the problem.

2. Solve the Problem in Front of You

Do not try to fix everything at once. Fix the immediate problem by working with what you know and what you can see. The temptation to solve everything at once leads to analysis paralysis. Instead, act with precision where you have clarity.

Example: In a training exercise in a branch of the military many years ago, a team was abseiling down some particularly slippery cliffs. One of the teammates lost his footing and slipped five metres down the cliff face. He froze; nothing would move. An old sergeant came down the cliff face and stopped next to him.

"I can't move, I'm scared. It's too far down, I'm going to fall," said the soldier.

The sergeant calmly told him to describe what he could see—his hands, his boots, the ropes, and the equipment. Making small changes, one at a time and fixing the immediate problem in front of him, and not thinking about the weather, the height they were, or the bigger picture, the two of them slowly and safely descended to the base of the cliff.

That moment wasn't just about survival but a lesson in focus, presence, and trust. Problem-solving starts where you are, not where you wish you were.

3. Now, Look Up, and See the Bigger Picture

When the immediate problems are being fixed, it's important to look up and make sure that you understand how the problem arose and also that your minor fixes are not creating new problems for yourself. A form of predictive analysis, risk management, and forward planning is key at this point. Short-term solutions may provide temporary relief, but without understanding the broader context, they risk becoming tomorrow's new problems.

Remember, at the heart of problem solving is to fix it and to prevent it from happening again (see Rule 5!). Sustainable solutions come from addressing causes, not just consequences.

Example: In the previous example, the immediate problem was getting the soldier safely down the cliff face, but the bigger picture issues were around using this as a training exercise at that time. Had the soldiers been trained on the equipment properly? Was the selection process appropriate for the soldiers to join the team? Was it a problem with the individual taking part who froze, or the process of training? These factors should be considered. Only by zooming out can a leader see whether the environment created the failure or merely exposed it.

4. Evaluate Results and Learn

Evaluate the effectiveness of your solution after implementation. Did it correct the issue? Did it meet your expectations? What were the unilateral results? Reflection is not optional—it's part of the leadership loop. Use this evaluation to learn about and improve your problem-solving skills and the power of your solutions. By taking time to assess what worked and what didn't, you not only strengthen your strategy but also build a sharper sense of judgment for the future.

5. Embrace Continuous Improvement

Problem-solving is a process. Accept a continuous learning mindset—always looking for better ways to identify and overcome challenges. Encourage your team to spot problems and offer solutions. Create a culture of learning and innovation where challenges are perceived as opportunities for growth and development. A good leader doesn't solve every problem—they empower others to become problem-solvers themselves.

And, of course, utilise technology as appropriate. Artificial Intelligence and its uses are accelerating at pace and are incredibly helpful in problem-solving. However, problem-solving is a human skill that can use AI and not vice versa. Machines can process data, but people must still interpret meaning, manage nuance, and drive solutions with empathy and context.

Problem Solving in Action: Real-World Examples

I have always believed that "all problems could be solved, the issue is the price of solving." It is a mentality that's enabled me to address challenges with determination, imagination, and the desire to find solutions no matter what. It's not a question of 'can it be done?'—it's a question of 'what will it take?' Some examples of how I used the rule in real-life situations:

The Celebrity Entry Challenge

As a young nightclub bouncer, I remember having a celebrity show up with an entourage expecting immediate entry. But the club was packed, last entry had passed, oh—and I did not actually know who the celebrity was. So I refused entry. He said, "Don't you know who I am? I'm XXXXXXX." My response was, "And I'm the doorman—and you're not coming in." In hindsight, it was a little rude, and it may have made things a bit worse. But in the moment, I was simply doing my job, with limited information and a policy to uphold.

The situation was tense. The celebrity was getting more agitated, and so was his entourage. Phone calls were made from the payphone across the street. (This story pre-dates mobile phones.) The nightclub owner, the press, and more senior entourage were called.

One of his security team approached the door and was aggressive towards the door staff, which resulted in a minor altercation. This was all getting out of hand, and it was clear that someone needed to back down before it got to the point where nobody could.

The end result was a combination of apologies all around—from the celebrity's team, the door staff, management—and lots of happy, smiling pictures of the celebrity with management, the door staff, and clubgoers, which, of course, ended up in the press. The tension was defused, the club's image was preserved, and the incident was turned into an unexpected PR opportunity.

But what is the cost, I hear you cry? A bit of personal pride, perhaps. Backing down from a stated position without being asked to, and volunteering an apology when people didn't think I needed to. It cost me a little ego, but I gained a lot in the outcome. That's often the price of a solution—small concessions that prevent larger consequences.

Lessons Learned

These examples and many others throughout my professional career illustrate the effectiveness of my problem-solving rule. Accepting that all problems are solvable has enabled me to deal with challenges with confidence, imagination, and dedication to get answers, no matter the price. It's a mindset that refuses to be blocked by frustration or circumstance.

This mindset has produced successful outcomes, but has also shown me leadership, negotiation, and the need to always consider the human factor when dealing with situations. It's a lesson in how even the most complicated issues can be resolved with critical thinking, ingenuity, and an appetite for attempting unconventional solutions. Ultimately, the goal isn't perfection—it's progress. And progress only happens when you're willing to confront problems head-on, break them down, and trust that there's always a way forward.

Chapter 6
Rule 4: "Telling Someone About an Issue Does Not Make It Their Issue"

Ownership: The Mark of a Leader

Telling someone about an issue doesn't make it their headache—this rule, perhaps more than any other, reflects my leadership philosophy and responsibility. It's a principle I have witnessed being violated numerous times—in the military and boardroom, raucous nightclubs, or even in the high-stakes world of business finance. It doesn't matter the environment—the pattern is the same: people report the problem and then back away from it, as if passing the message absolves them of further duty. People point out problems, they sound alarms, and they delegate responsibility. But true leaders take ownership. They're the ones who say, "I got this," and act upon it.

Taking ownership is not about ego, control, or trying to be heroic. It's about understanding that identifying a problem is only the first step. The real work is finding solutions and making changes. It's about realizing that problems—whatever their source or complexity—become your problems the instant you become aware of them. Whether a team member made a mistake, a process was inefficient, or an unexpected external challenge appeared. Leadership means stepping into discomfort, not sidestepping it. Leaders do not avoid responsibility; they accept it.

I see so many people escalate things and by doing so, think it has moved off their desk, and thus, that they have done everything that is needed. This is not the case. Just because you have sent an email doesn't mean that suddenly you turn oblivious of the entire situation. The chain of responsibility doesn't end with a CC line. Ownership means following through, not forwarding out.

There is a famous interview with Barack Obama after he left office that I often share and quote. He says that throughout his career, he has met literally thousands of people who have been brilliant at articulating a problem or explaining why something won't work. He says that all he wants is for someone to say, "I got this." No matter how small or complex the matter is, just wanting someone to step up and fix it. It's a powerful leadership filter. Talk less about the roadblocks and more about how you'll clear the path. People need to be part of the solution and not just pass the problem on.

Why is taking ownership so crucial for effective leadership?

1. Empowerment and Action

You take ownership of a problem, and you are empowered to act. You become an active problem seeker instead of a passive observer. Stop complaining, pointing fingers, or blaming, and start doing something about it. This proactive approach is needed to move forward, get results, and create a culture of solution-oriented thinking. Ownership breeds movement. It's the pivot point from reaction to resolution. When people see leaders step forward instead of stepping aside, it energizes a team to do the same, igniting a pulsating energy within the entire network.

2. Building Trust and Respect

Taking ownership demonstrates responsibility and accountability, which builds trust and respect among others. When you consistently step up to address challenges, your team and colleagues recognize your commitment and reliability. They see you as someone they can count on to take action, not delegate or deflect! You become the person who doesn't just point out leaks—you grab a bucket or a patch to fix. This builds confidence and a culture of collaboration and mutual support—everybody feels empowered to make a difference. And that, in turn, reduces blame culture and increases shared responsibility.

3. Developing Problem-Solving Skills

Taking ownership gives you great opportunities to practice problem-solving. By actively tackling challenges, you learn how to analyze situations, find causes, evaluate solutions, and apply strategies. It becomes a muscle—the more you use it, the sharper it gets. This helps you navigate difficult situations, make informed decisions, and change with the times. You not only get better at solving problems, you get faster at recognizing patterns, anticipating risks, and responding under pressure.

4. A Culture of Accountability

Leaders who take ownership consistently set an example for their teams. They build a culture where everyone can take ownership, contribute to solutions, and learn from failures. This builds ownership and accountability, creating a more engaged, proactive, and productive workforce. People stop hiding mistakes and camouflaging their errors—they start fixing them. It creates a climate where people dare to fail, innovate, and strive for excellence, knowing they will be supported even when they stumble. Because when leadership owns outcomes, teams feel safe enough to take meaningful risks.

5. Driving Positive Change

Ultimately, ownership is about driving change. By actively addressing challenges and seeking out solutions, you help your team, organization, and world improve. You become an agent of social change—inspiring others to act, take responsibility, and make a positive change. The ripple effect of ownership can be transformative. One person stepping up can elevate the entire standard of performance around them. You demonstrate that leadership is about far more than authority and titles—it's about striving to improve things, influencing outcomes, and making a difference in the world. And that difference starts not with permission, but with initiative.

Dangers of the Imaginary Someone

One of the biggest barriers to ownership is the ubiquitous mindset of the "imaginary someone." How often have you heard phrases like "Somebody should look into that" or "Someone needs to fix that"? This dependence on an anonymous, unnamed “someone” creates a diffusion culture where everyone thinks someone else will take responsibility. It's the illusion of delegation without the reality of action. It is dangerous apathy—where people give up contributing to solutions, where possibilities get missed, and where progress is delayed not by complexity, but by passivity.

The imaginary someone is an illusion. It causes problems to fester, chances to be missed, and potential solutions to be lost. When responsibility is passed into a vacuum, no one steps up because no one knows they should. It breeds complacency, undermines accountability, and blocks innovation. It creates a climate where people feel powerless to change, disengage from their work, and eventually lose the initiative to make a difference. Worse still, it normalizes inertia—because when no one owns the problem, no one feels the urgency to solve it.

We have to combat that mindset as leaders. "Someone" must be replaced by "I." We must involve our teams in the solution, not just as observers of the issue, but as active participants in resolving it. Ownership isn't a title; it's a posture. We need a culture where everyone can see problems, suggest solutions, and do something about them—even if it's a small step in the right direction.

The Power of "I"

In my leadership journey, I've learned that changing "someone" to "I" can be transformative. It puts the emphasis on action instead of blame and delegation. It breaks inertia, silences excuses, and replaces vagueness with resolve. It inspires people to take charge and make a difference. It gives people ownership and accountability for the team and the organization, because they begin to see themselves not just as cogs in a machine, but as drivers of change.

Not that you must do all of it yourself. Effective delegation still matters—but it should be accompanied by clear expectations, defined roles, and shared accountability. When you delegate, you do more than just hand over responsibility; you extend trust and invite growth. You're encouraging someone to take ownership and learn how they solve problems for themselves, and in doing so, you're building their capacity to lead in the future.

True leadership isn't about doing more—it's about enabling more. And when people see that you're not just delegating tasks but empowering ownership, they become more engaged, more resourceful, and more committed to the outcomes.

The Filter System

Roles and responsibilities: I often use a filter system with my teams. This system teaches people how to assess their autonomy when addressing various issues and when to escalate problems to higher leadership levels. It helps them take ownership of issues within the scope of their responsibility and opens up pathways for more complex or critical issues. The filter is not about restricting decision-making—it's about clarifying it.

The filter system provides a framework for decision-making and accountability—while ensuring critical issues get sufficient attention and oversight. It gives people the confidence to act within bounds, knowing they're supported, not scrutinized. It creates trust and transparency where everyone knows their part in problem-solving and feels empowered to contribute to the solution rather than wait for direction. Clarity, after all, is the foundation of action.

Communication and Delegation: Essential Tools for Ownership

Taking ownership of the problem does not mean solving it by yourself. Effective leadership involves assigning tasks and responsibilities to others so they can share the load. But delegating without clear communication can cause confusion, frustration and, ultimately, failure to take ownership. Clarity in expectations transforms delegation from task distribution to capability-building.

The best leaders communicate not just what needs to be done, but why it matters, how success will be measured, and where support will come from. When people understand the broader goal and feel trusted to own their part of the process, they move from compliance to commitment. Delegation then becomes a strategic act, not of relieving pressure from the top, but of distributing power throughout the team.

Here are a few tips on how to communicate and delegate so your team can take ownership:

1. Clear and Concise Communication

When delegating or communicating about problems, use simple language. Do not use jargon or ambiguity that could confuse things. Identify the problem, desired outcome, and constraints and considerations. Clarity removes the guesswork and puts everyone on a common footing. It's the first step in setting your team up for success.

Example: Don't say, "We should increase our social media presence." Give specific instructions: I need you to grow our Instagram followers by 15% next quarter with content and ad campaigns. This removes ambiguity and gives your team something measurable to aim for and further shapes you as a person who knows the ins and outs of the company's statistics.

2. Active Listening

Communication is a two-way street. Listen to what your team members have to point out, and provide ideas and feedback. Respect their points of view and promote open dialogue. This builds trust and understanding and leads to cooperative problem-solving. Listening isn't passive—it's leadership in action. When people feel heard, they become more invested in the outcome.

Example: Ask questions when a team member is concerned about a project and listen. This tells them you value their input and want to collaborate on solutions. Even better, paraphrase their concern to confirm your understanding and respond thoughtfully, not reactively.

3. Defined Roles and Responsibilities

Define roles and responsibilities for the team. Ensure that everyone understands their role and where their job fits within the bigger picture. This clarity avoids confusion, increases accountability, and empowers people to take responsibility for their work. When people understand the "why" behind their role, they perform with more ownership and intent.

Example: Assign a project and spell out each phase's team roles, responsibilities, and deadlines. This helps everybody remain on the same page and on target. When responsibilities are outlined clearly, individuals become accountable without needing reminders.

4. Appropriate Delegation

Delegate tasks that match people's skills and interests. This allows them to play to their strengths, grow, and contribute to the team. Avoid delegating tasks that they cannot complete or that involve specialized knowledge that they lack. Misaligned delegation doesn't just cause frustration—it damages confidence and momentum. It proves another important aspect of competent leadership which is to know our team. A competent team leader would know the strengths and weaknesses of his team and would delegate accordingly.

Example: If a team member is a data analyst, delegate data interpretation and reporting tasks. And if another team member is a great writer, have that person write your presentations or other communications. Use strengths strategically and allow room for skill-building where possible.

5. Ensure Resources and Support Are Available

Assign tasks, but make sure your team members have the data, tools, training, and/or mentorship they need to succeed. Don't just hand them off to them. Give them the tools and support to take ownership and achieve results. Delegating without equipping is setting people up to fail—and responsible leaders don't do that.

Example: If you delegate something requiring a particular software program, ensure the team member has that software and any training they need to use it properly. Support doesn't mean micromanaging—it means enabling.

6. Regular Check-Ins and Feedback

Communicate frequently with team members—check-ins, status reports, and feedback—to monitor their progress, offer direction, and resolve issues or concerns. Regular communication also shows you remain committed to their success. It signals that you care about the process, not just the outcome.

Example: Hold regular team meetings and individual check-ins to review project progress, give feedback on performance, and offer support and guidance if necessary. These touchpoints become opportunities to recalibrate, refocus, and reinforce commitment.

7. Recognize and Celebrate Successes

Celebrate successes when team members take ownership and produce positive results. This reinforces their contributions and increases morale and commitment to taking initiative and solving problems. Acknowledgement fuels engagement. People repeat what gets recognized.

Example: Publicly recognize achievements at team meetings, send congratulatory emails, or give small rewards or incentives for outstanding performance. Simple recognition often carries more weight than we think—it affirms value and motivates further ownership.

8. Embrace Constructive Feedback

Encourage open feedback. Give constructive criticism when needed, but be open to feedback from your team. This creates an environment for learning where everyone is comfortable sharing ideas, addressing concerns, and striving for improvement. True feedback culture isn't top-down—it's circular.

Example: Set up a space for team feedback on your leadership style, communication approach, or delegation methods. Accept their suggestions and adjust your strategy accordingly. Nothing builds respect like a leader who listens, learns, and evolves.

Implementing these communication and delegation strategies enables your team to take responsibility, solve problems efficiently, and contribute to the organization. Clare's communication, clearly defined roles, and ongoing support foster a collaborative climate where all feel valued, respected, and accountable for their contributions. When leadership leads with clarity and care, teams respond with commitment and capability.

Addressing Issues within a Team: A Leader's Guide

Teams are dynamic entities of people with viewpoints, skills, and different personalities, but this diversity can also create conflicts, miscommunications, and challenges that need to be navigated and led well. Leadership here means more than managing—it means mediating, facilitating, and guiding people through differences toward shared outcomes.

How to approach and deal with issues within a team to create ownership, accountability and collaborative problem-solving:

1. Create a Safe Space for Open Communication

Make it comfortable for team members to express concerns, ideas, and feedback without fear of retribution. Stress the importance of respectful dialogue and active listening. People speak up when they feel safe, and when they do, you get to the heart of issues faster.

Example: Hold regular team meetings where everyone can contribute. Make mistakes "an opportunity to learn," not a cause for punishment; adopt a no-blame policy. Lead by example—share your own learning moments and normalize the idea that even leaders don't have all the answers all the time.

2. Identify and Acknowledge the Issue

When a problem occurs within the team, don't just ignore it or hope it disappears. Identify and acknowledge the issue. Address it directly and constructively. This shows you're committed to resolving disputes and creating a good working environment. Avoiding a problem does not neutralize it—it usually makes it worse and more personal.

Example: If there's tension between two team members, speak privately with each member and then bring them together for a constructive conversation. If there's a process inefficiency holding productivity back, admit the problem in a group meeting and have everyone help you find solutions. Your willingness to face issues transparently sets the tone for the entire team.

3. **Gather Perspectives and Information**

Before jumping to decisions or imposing solutions, gather perspectives and information from everyone involved. This helps you understand the causes, identify biases or muddled messages, and develop better solutions. The full story rarely lives in just one place—ask, listen, and validate before moving forward.

Example: When disagreements about a project's direction arise, consult all team members and anyone outside the team who may be invested in the project's outcome. This broader perspective can reveal the reasons for disagreement and help you find solutions that satisfy everyone. Sometimes, the friction isn't about the task—it's about assumptions that were never voiced.

4. Collaborative Problem-Solving

Encourage team participation. Facilitate brainstorming, open dialogue, and ownership of the issue. This collaborative approach gains buy-in, builds team cohesion, and delivers more long-term solutions. When people help shape the solution, they're more likely to commit to its success.

Example: If there's a communication breakdown in the team, host a workshop to identify causes and brainstorm solutions. This may include new communication tools, clear communication protocols, or training in active listening and dispute resolution. Let the team feel they're not just fixing a problem—they're improving the culture.

5. Focus on Solutions, Not Blame

Do not assign blame or dwell on past mistakes. Rather, look for solutions that fix the present issue and prevent it from occurring again. This is more positive and productive. Blame drains energy—solution-building restores it.

Example: When missing a project deadline, do not focus on who did it. Instead, analyze why the delay happened, pinpoint improvement areas, and plan to avoid it again. When the team sees that missteps are treated as learning opportunities, accountability becomes a shared value rather than a fear-driven response.

6. Clearly Define Roles and Responsibilities

Once a solution is identified, define the roles and responsibilities involved in implementing it. Ensure everyone knows their contribution and where their work fits into the bigger picture. This clarity enables accountability and smoother execution. Ambiguity is the enemy of follow-through.

Example: If the team decides to implement a new project management tool, assign specific roles for researching different options, evaluating their features, and leading the implementation process. Ownership increases when individuals can see where their efforts lead and how they impact the whole.

7. Provide Support and Resources

Ensure your team members have the support and resources to implement the solution successfully. This could be providing training, tools, mentors, or other resources. Show dedication to their success by helping them overcome obstacles and attain their goals. Support isn't a luxury—it's part of enabling success.

Example: If the team chooses to use a new communication protocol, train the team on the new system, provide ongoing support for questions or challenges, and make resources available to help with the transition. When you invest in their success, they begin to invest more fully in the outcome.

8. Monitor Progress and Provide Feedback

Regularly check the team's progress in resolving the issue. Give constructive feedback, acknowledge achievements, and address challenges and setbacks. This ongoing communication shows you care about the team and helps ensure the solution gets implemented. Leadership is not about checking out once the plan is in place—it's about staying connected until the goal is reached.

Example: Schedule regular check-ins to review progress, provide feedback on performance, and provide help or advice as needed. Celebrate milestones and individual contributions to reinforce good behavior and keep momentum going. Progress is more sustainable when it's recognized and redirected when necessary.

9. Evaluate Results and Learn from Experience

Once the problem is fixed, evaluate the results. Was the solution effective in fixing the problem? What happened that was not intended? What are the lessons derived? Use this evaluation to inform your preparation for future challenges and build a culture of improvement and learning. Every resolution leaves a trail of wisdom—if you're willing to trace it.

Example: After implementing the new communication protocol, conduct a survey to get team feedback on how it went. Analyze results, spot improvement areas, and make adjustments where needed to improve communication and collaboration within the team. Good teams solve problems—great teams grow stronger from solving them.

Chapter 7
Rule 5: "Anyone Can Make a Mistake. Twice is Stupidity. Three Times is Incompetence

Learning from Mistakes: The Foundation of Growth

Anyone can make a mistake. Such a straightforward statement is the foundation of my fifth rule, reflecting an important fact about human experience. We are flawed beings—we make judgment, attention, and calculation mistakes. Mistakes happen, especially in the fast-moving and unpredictable business and leadership worlds. However, no matter how seasoned or intelligent one may be, error is an inevitable part of any dynamic decision-making process, and denying that reality only fosters rigidity and fear.

The real test of a person, especially a leader, is not how they can avoid making mistakes but how they can learn from them—how to grow from them—and how to use those experiences to improve their performance in the future. True growth begins the moment we stop shielding ourselves from discomfort and begin confronting our shortcomings with honesty and resolve.

To learn this requires a culture of accountability. Accountability involves neither blame nor punishment. It means owning up to your actions and consequences, good or bad. It is about creating an environment where mistakes can become opportunities for growth and not personal failures. Such a culture encourages transparency and deters the instinct to hide errors, fostering openness, psychological safety, and collective responsibility.

In a culture of accountability, people are encouraged to admit their errors, find out what went wrong, and make plans to prevent them again. This creates a feedback loop where learning and improvement are embedded. As people begin to realize that accountability is not punitive but developmental, they grow more confident in facing their weaknesses and transforming them into strengths.

However, the critical piece here is that you must learn from mistakes. I believe that if someone makes the same mistake twice, then they clearly didn't do the learning part, and that is, to be honest, stupid. If they repeat the same mistake a third time, then they are showing that they cannot learn from their mistakes, and the flip side of that is that they are not willing to try, develop, or learn and grow. In which case, I don't believe they are the best person to have in the team. Mistakes are understandable; they happen, but so must the learning and improvement. After all, the work needs to be done. Repeated failure without reflection reveals not just a gap in skill but a gap in attitude—an unwillingness to evolve, which poses a greater threat to the team than the mistake itself.

So Why Is Learning from Mistakes Critical to Leadership?

1. Growth and Development

We learn best from mistakes. Their results can tell us about ourselves—what exactly our inadequacies are, exactly where our blind spots are, and exactly where we can improve. Analyzing our errors helps us understand ourselves, our decisions, and what makes us successful and fail. This is necessary for professional and personal growth—to improve our skills and techniques and become better leaders. It forces us to slow down, assess our reasoning, and reconstruct our approach from the ground up, leading to a deeper mastery that mere success cannot offer.

2. Innovation and Adaptability

Acceptance of making mistakes promotes innovation and adaptation. We are much more prone to take chances, try new ideas, and do more with what we have whenever we don't fear failure. This creates an environment of experimentation, learning, and adaptation that drives progress. Without room for trial and error, creativity dies at the altar of perfectionism, and organizations stagnate instead of evolving.

3. Building Resilience

Mistakes may be setbacks, but they need not be defeats. Learning from our errors builds resilience to overcome challenges and setbacks. We see mistakes as opportunities for growth and become more positive and optimistic about things, realizing that even our failures can lead to our ultimate success. Resilience is not about avoiding hardship but becoming skilled at navigating it, and mistakes are often the training ground where this emotional muscle is built.

4. Strengthening Trust and Relationships

Recognizing mistakes and taking responsibility builds trust and relationships. Leaders who admit their mistakes are humble and committed to learning and improvement. It encourages vulnerability and transparency—people can take risks, exchange ideas, and learn from one another. This openness dismantles hierarchies of fear and replaces them with shared accountability, reinforcing a culture where collaboration outweighs self-protection.

5. Preventing Future Errors

Most likely, the biggest advantage of learning from mistakes is avoiding them down the road. Analyzing our faltering behaviour, finding root causes, and correcting causes reduces the risk of repeating the same error. This creates an efficient and effective organization where learning and improvement are continuous processes. Every misstep becomes a data point, a guidepost that strengthens systems, sharpens judgment, and tightens execution across the board.

The Importance of Structured Learning

Although many life lessons should be learned by error and trial, structured learning is also important. Structured learning can be formal education, professional training, or mentoring programs. These forms of learning provide frameworks and foundational knowledge that serve as a reliable source when navigating the uncertain terrain of real-world leadership challenges.

I've learned much from my journey—from structured learning to learning by experience. I had a solid foundation in financial principles and practices through my formal accounting training. I learned leadership, risk management, and human behaviour through my military, bodyguard, and nightclub bouncer experiences. Each phase, though distinct in setting and expectation, offered a layer of depth that theory alone could never fully provide, forcing me to apply principles in unpredictable, often high-stakes environments.

Structured learning mixed with practical experience has shaped my approach to leadership—to put theory into practice and adjust strategies based on lessons learned. The balance between academic rigor and real-life adaptation has proven essential: where structure teaches discipline, experience demands flexibility.

Embracing a Growth Mindset

To learn from failures, it's important to have a growth attitude and believe in our ability to progress with hard work. A growth mindset encourages taking risks, persevering through setbacks, and recognizing effort as the path to mastery. It transforms the fear of failure into a hunger for development, allowing leaders to see struggle not as a sign of weakness but as evidence of movement.

Leaders who cultivate a growth attitude in their teams encourage learning and improvement. They promote experimentation and development, and view failures as opportunities for achievement rather than obstacles to progress. This environment fosters resilience, invites open dialogue, and builds a collective appetite for growth that endures beyond individual moments of success or failure.

Learning from Mistakes: The Foundation of Growth

My journey has not been flawless. It's been a winding path with many turns, bumps, and drops, and I stumbled, fell, and even face-planted. But every misstep and failure has been a teacher, shaping my leadership style and decision-making process and teaching me to learn from experience. Some lessons arrived gently, others came like a punch to the gut, but each one etched itself into my understanding in a way no lecture ever could.

It's easy to laud the successes and gloss over the failures, but in those moments of imperfection, of things not going to plan, we learn and grow. A few stories from my own journey illustrate this principle in action: experiences where pain, humility, and reflection converged into valuable transformation.

The Jiu-Jitsu Lesson

My eldest and my youngest sons started learning Jiu-Jitsu. They are both natural sports kids with a competitive streak and a drive to succeed. They both became very good at the sport and showed natural talent, and worked hard to learn what is an incredibly complex sport. Both entered their first tournaments and faced strong competition. Unfortunately, they both lost their first fight in their first tournament. My eldest tapped out; something he swore he would never do—sometimes in life we all have to tap out—and the youngest lost on points.

The disappointment was felt. They both walked off the mats disappointed and somewhat dejected. No words would help. There was a heavy silence, the kind that sits between a bruised ego and the first glimmer of acceptance, and as a parent, it was difficult to watch.

My wife, with more experience in tournaments and sports, and a great source of inspiration and wisdom for me, taught me a lesson. On the way home, she told them both that she understood their disappointment but tried to frame the experience as either winning or learning, and often both. Her words didn't erase the sting of loss, but they gently redirected the focus from failure to reflection, and eventually, to renewal.

Her words really touched me. They encapsulated the essence of my fifth rule. Not to avoid mistakes altogether, but to use them as learning experiences. Understanding failure isn't the complete opposite of success—it is simply a step toward success. That insight, simple yet profound, is what separates temporary defeat from long-term growth.

My youngest took those words to heart, thankfully. He analyzed his match—pinpointed where he stumbled, what techniques he needed to perfect, and where he made strategic errors. He returned to training, determined to work on his weaknesses, fine-tuning his craft, and becoming stronger mentally. He learned from his loss and adjusted his strategy. Each day on the mat became a form of redemption, and with every drill, he rebuilt not just his technique but his confidence.

My eldest decided that the sport was not for him, his competitive mindset taking him a little too far down the path of 'if you're not the best, then what's the point'. Not every story is a successful one. But we learn as we grow as parents. Sometimes the lesson isn't about perseverance but about self-awareness—understanding when to pivot and respecting that choice without judgment.

The Sport of Rugby

Rugby, to me, is a sport of great humility. Teams are respectful to match officials, unlike other sports like football. Players can be of all shapes and sizes, and respect is earned. A kicker kicks, and a prop pushes. No fish are judged for their inability to climb a tree. That egalitarian spirit—the idea that everyone has a role and value, regardless of form—is what drew me to the game and kept me there.

But after a gap of about 10 years from schoolboy to adult rugby, I found myself playing again, and as a prop. I listened and learnt from the older players, and despite my strength and power, I was frequently humbled in those early years by wily old guys, smaller than me but with tricks that took me a long time to learn. Many a game, I would come off the pitch feeling like I had been turned inside out. It wasn't just about brute strength; it was about nuance, timing, and understanding the subtle physics of movement and balance.

In the after-match debrief (drinking in the bar after the game), I would always make a point of chatting with the opposition prop who had destroyed me and asking him how he did it. In my later playing years and now as a coach, I passed on that knowledge to other younger players. Helping them to learn from their mistakes and improve. There's a quiet dignity in passing down what once humbled you, offering it not as a shield, but as a stepping stone for someone else's journey.

The Communication Breakdown

In my early days in business, I had to oversee a project, pretty much for the first time. We had a tight deadline and some very demanding stakeholders. In my focus on meeting the deliverables and ensuring that every "I" was dotted and every "t" crossed, I inadvertently created an environment where open communication and feedback were stifled. What I thought was diligence and precision was, in fact, rigidity—an atmosphere where execution took precedence over collaboration, and silence became the safer choice for many in the team.

Sensing my intensity and focus on efficiency, team members hesitated to raise concerns, ask for clarification, or offer alternative perspectives. They feared doing so would be perceived as weakness, incompetence, or lack of commitment. This caused a communication bottleneck as important information was withheld, miscommunications developed, and errors multiplied. Small issues that could have been easily resolved if they had surfaced early grew into larger operational setbacks because the team was overwhelmed by silence and hesitation.

It was a delay in the project timeline, a scramble to correct mistakes, and general team frustration and anxiety. Recognizing my part in the communication breakdown, I took responsibility. I apologized and called a team meeting. I said my focus on efficiency created an environment where open communications were discouraged, and everyone should feel comfortable sharing their views, concerns, and ideas. It was a difficult moment, acknowledging that my well-intentioned intensity had become a barrier, but it was a necessary first step in regaining credibility.

I could say that I fixed it immediately, but I did not. I had lost the trust of the team, and it took a shift in my mindset and some time for it to be seen to impact those individuals. Rebuilding trust wasn't about grand gestures or quick fixes—it was about consistency, humility, and making space for voices I had unintentionally quieted. Over time, small acknowledgments of contribution, openness to feedback, and a softening of my tone helped reset the dynamic.

That experience taught me a lesson about leadership and teamwork. It highlighted the need for clear and open communication, active listening, and a culture where everyone is valued, respected, and empowered to contribute their views and ideas. Effective leadership is not just about clarity of vision, but about the clarity of connection—ensuring people feel heard before they are instructed. That lesson has shaped how I approach communication and collaboration ever since—that even the best intentions can backfire on a leader and cause friction in teamwork. Intent without awareness is insufficient; it is through reflection and adjustment that real growth takes root.

The Lessons of Failure

These stories and thousands more throughout my career have taught me to learn from mistakes. Though painful, disappointing, and embarrassing, failure can be a valuable teacher, giving insights and perspectives that success cannot provide. While success often affirms our current approach, failure interrogates it, offering lessons with sharper edges and longer-lasting impact.

In those moments of imperfection, when we stumble and fall, we learn, grow, and develop the resilience and wisdom that make effective leadership possible. Each setback becomes a seed of insight, each embarrassment a moment of introspection, and each correction a stepping stone to better judgment and deeper empathy.

Preventing Mistakes and Fostering Continuous Improvement

Learning from mistakes is good, but still, it's better to prevent them altogether. While errors offer fertile ground for insight, a proactive stance—rooted in anticipation, preparation, and reflection—significantly reduces their occurrence and consequence. A culture of continuous improvement requires preventative strategies that minimize errors, promote learning, and nurture a mindset of ongoing development.

Here are some key strategies to avoid making the same mistakes again and build a culture of continuous improvement:

1. Establish Clear Processes and Procedures

Clearly defined processes and procedures promote consistency and efficiency and reduce the chance of errors caused by ambiguity or lack of guidance. When workflows are transparent and expectations are explicit, teams are far less likely to falter due to misinterpretation or miscommunication. Create checklists for critical jobs and standard operating procedures for routine activities—document essential workflow elements.

Example: Create a new employee onboarding process that outlines steps, key resources, and expectations for the role. This assures consistency in training and eliminates errors due to a lack of knowledge or direction.

2. Encourage Open Communication and Feedback

Create an environment where team members can express concerns, questions, and feedback without fear of judgment or reprisal. Open communication channels allow early detection of potential problems before they escalate into larger, costlier issues. When people feel safe to speak up, silent risks surface early, giving leaders the chance to address them while they are still manageable.

Example: Hold regular feedback sessions where the team can share thoughts and ideas—good and bad. Encourage constructive criticism and a place for dialogue.

3. Promote Knowledge Sharing and Collaboration

Encourage knowledge sharing and collaborative work amongst the team. Give team members opportunities to share knowledge, experience, and ideas for solutions. This collective intelligence prevents mistakes because the team has different expertise and perspectives. The intersection of diverse insights often reveals blind spots and innovative approaches that no individual could discover alone.

Example: Create a knowledge base where teammates can document learnings, best practices, and resources. Organize regular workshops or trainings so people can share their expertise and gain from one another.

4. Provide Adequate Training and Development

Invest in training and developmental programs so your team members know how to perform their roles. Regular training updates and professional development opportunities avoid mistakes caused by outdated knowledge and skill gaps. An evolving business demands evolving capabilities, and training is the bridge between current competence and future readiness.

Example: Train employees on new technologies, industry best practices, and applicable regulations. Offer professional certifications or advanced learning.

5. Implement Quality Control Measures

Introduce quality control measures throughout your processes to catch errors before they affect the final result. These may include peer reviews, checklists, automated checks, or regular audits. By embedding quality assurance at multiple checkpoints, you create a safeguard that reinforces consistency without compromising agility.

Example: Have all reports or presentations peer-reviewed before being sent to clients or stakeholders. This allows early identification of errors or inconsistent work.

6. Accept Technology and Automation

Use technology and automation to reduce manual errors and increase efficiency. This may involve software solutions for data analysis, project management, or communication.

Technology, when aligned with human judgment, becomes a powerful enabler of accuracy, consistency, and speed.

Example: Track progress, assign tasks, and monitor deadlines with project management software to reduce the risk of errors due to miscommunication and missed deadlines.

7. Conduct Root Cause Analysis

When mistakes happen, do a root cause analysis to determine the reasons behind the error. This means going beyond the immediate cause to identify underlying systemic problems or gaps in process design. Without this depth of analysis, quick fixes only mask recurring issues and delay true resolution.

Example: Correct incorrect information a client gave a customer service representative, but don't reprimand the person. Find out what caused the error. Was it a lack of training, an outdated knowledge base, or a customer service issue?

8. Implement Corrective Actions

Based on root cause analysis, take corrective actions to fix problems and avoid error recurrence. This could be updating processes, adding training, or adopting new tools or technologies. Real improvement comes not from pointing out what went wrong, but from having the courage to reshape the systems that allowed it to happen.

Example: If a customer service error is caused by outdated information in the knowledge base, update the information and train all customer service representatives.

9. Foster a Culture of Learning

Promote learning in your culture. Encourage experimentation, growth, and development, and reward those who initiate and improve. By normalizing learning, you remove the stigma from failure and shift focus toward progress.

Example: Create a "lesson learned" database where the team can document successes and failures. Share these learnings frequently to spread knowledge and avoid repeating mistakes.

10. Lead by Example

As you lead, model the behaviour you would like to see in your team. Accept continuous learning, own your mistakes, and show commitment to continuous improvement. Your actions speak louder than words, and your team will buy into a culture of continuous improvement when you're actively involved. Consistency between what you say and what you do is the cornerstone of credibility, and credibility is what sustains long-term growth.

Using these strategies, you can create a climate where mistakes are seen as lessons to be learned and growth, not failures to yourself. This makes for a more resilient, adaptive, and innovative organization where continuous improvement is the expected standard, and everybody strives to improve. In such a culture, excellence is not a destination but a habit, reinforced daily by a shared commitment to getting better, together.

Chapter 8
Rule 6: "Do What You Care About and Care About What You Do"

Passion and Purpose: The Heart and Soul of Leadership

Okay, so let's talk about passion and purpose. Those words get tossed around daily but aren't just empty buzzwords. They're the real deal—the heart and soul of excellent leadership. They're not corporate jargon to sprinkle into presentations; they're the very elements that make leadership human, inspiring, and sustainable over the long haul.

Think about it. Have you ever worked a job you disliked? Did you get out of bed every morning and count the minutes until the day ended? Yup, it's not a recipe for inspiration, is it? Drudgery kills momentum, saps creativity, and makes even the smallest task feel like an uphill battle.

Now, imagine the opposite. A job you love that gets you fired up and ready for the day's challenges. That's the power of passion. The fuel we use is the spark that ignites our creativity and decision-making compass. It pulls us forward even when the terrain is rough, acting as a kind of emotional momentum that transforms obligation into opportunity.

And purpose? That is our "why": we do what we do. This sense of meaning gives us meaning in our work and belongs to something more important than ourselves. We lead with purpose so others can follow and do extraordinary things. Purpose turns our daily grind into a mission; it gives significance to the sleepless nights and the hard decisions because we believe they're in service of something greater.

I have always said that to be happy at work, you need four things:

1. Find something you're good at
2. Find something you enjoy
3. Find great people to work with
4. Find a way to get paid for it

I have been exceptionally lucky in my career and have had a number of jobs where I have had all four. Enjoying things and even loving them and being passionate about your work, your life, and the people in it is critical to being successful. When these elements align, work becomes not just a means of income but a platform for fulfillment, contribution, and joy—and that's when leadership starts to flourish.

So why are passion and purpose important in leadership?

1. Motivation and Drive

Nobody wants to follow a guy who's just going through the motions. We want somebody enthusiastic about the work who believes in the team and drives us to be our best. That's where passion enters. It's not about theatrical energy or loud enthusiasm—it's about deeply held conviction that fuels action and inspires others to give more than they thought they could.

It is like having an inner engine that keeps us going in case things get hard and we are passionate about what we do. We are naturally driven to do much better, to be much better, and to conquer challenges not simply because we must do so but because we would like to. And that enthusiasm is infectious. It energizes our teams, creates a good work environment, and pushes everyone to do better. It's in the late-night brainstorming sessions, the small wins we celebrate together, and the confidence people develop when they see a leader who truly believes in the mission.

Think of a leader who is absolutely buzzing about their mission—whether it involves creating new technologies, providing outstanding customer service, or making a difference in the community. Their passion drives their team to work harder and think differently to achieve common goals.

2. Resilience and Perseverance

Leadership isn't easy—sometimes. There will be setbacks, challenges, and moments when you just want to slap your hands and say, "Forget it!" That's why purpose comes in. It's that invisible hand that steadies us when pressure mounts, reminding us that the work is worth doing even when it feels uphill.

It provides us with the strength to keep going when the going gets tough—having a definite purpose, having a reason for doing what we do. It's like having an anchor in a stormy sea. This commitment motivates our teams to tackle challenges with determination and confidence. It fosters a culture where obstacles aren't viewed as roadblocks but as necessary parts of the journey.

Imagine a leader motivated by something as simple as promoting sustainability, social justice, or improving healthcare outcomes. This motivates them to overcome obstacles, negotiate difficult situations, and focus on achieving goals despite criticism or setbacks. They lead not with force, but with direction, pulling others through the storm by the clarity of their vision.

3. Creativity and Innovation

Nobody wants to work where things stay the same and new ideas are censored. We want innovation, creativity, and the thrill of new possibilities. Here comes passion and purpose.

When we are truly involved in our work—whenever we really feel excited and purposeful about our work—our minds open to possibilities. We're more likely to think outside the box, question established wisdom, and find new solutions. This creates a creative thinking culture where everyone can contribute ideas and make things possible. It sparks a kind of collective curiosity, where challenges become puzzles and teams are energized by the freedom to explore.

Think of a leader passionate about developing new technologies or finding creative solutions for complex problems. Their enthusiasm drives their team to think, do new things, try new things, and see what else is possible. They don't just tolerate innovation—they demand it, nurture it, and live it out loud.

4. Authenticity and Trust

No one wants to follow a fake leader who's just a façade. We want somebody real, honest with themselves, and operating with integrity. Here comes passion and purpose.

If what we do reflects our beliefs and values, and we are enthusiastic about what we do, we come across as trustworthy and real. Authenticity isn't about being perfect; it's about being consistent—aligning what we say, what we do, and what we believe in a way that resonates with those around us.

That builds trust and respect with our teams, colleagues, and stakeholders. It creates space for honest conversations, stronger collaboration, and meaningful connections that endure beyond project deadlines or quarterly targets.

Imagine a leader who cares about team welfare and ethical business and demonstrates their value through action. This authenticity creates trust and respect—a safe workplace where everyone feels valued and respected. And when people feel safe, they feel seen; when they feel seen, they thrive.

5. Personal and Professional Fulfillment

We all want to feel fulfilled at work as if we are doing something useful. Here comes passion and purpose.

We feel satisfied and accomplished when we work in a way that reflects our values, excites us, and fulfils us. This accomplishment benefits us as individuals and our leadership effectiveness as well. Fulfilled leaders lead with more clarity, empathy, and conviction—and those qualities ripple outward, affecting culture, morale, and productivity.

When we are fulfilled in our work, we can influence and motivate others in a better way, which is good for any workplace. It's the difference between managing a team and building one—between overseeing tasks and shaping legacies.

For example, a leader who loves mentoring their team members to become better individuals and attain goals. This sense of purpose and fulfillment promotes their leadership effectiveness and creates a generative environment where everyone feels valued and empowered to succeed.

Finding Your Passion and Purpose

Now you are probably thinking, okay, so where do I find my purpose and passion in leadership? It's a journey to self-discovery, buddy. It takes reflection, introspection, and willingness to explore your values, interests, and aspirations. It is about determining what drives you, what type of world you wish to generate, and how to use your talents and gifts to get there. It's not a one-time epiphany; it's a slow uncovering of what truly matters to you, done through observation, discomfort, and honest evaluation.

This may include:

Identifying values: What are your most important principles? What kind of world do you want to create? So, what sort of leader would you want to become? When you understand your values clearly, they become non-negotiables—the quiet voice that steers your decisions even when no one's watching.

Exploring your interests: What activities do you enjoy? What topics excite you? What type of work causes me to feel energized and awake? Chances are, the things that make you lose track of time are pointing you directly toward your purpose—if you're paying attention.

Identifying strengths: What do you naturally do well? Which skills do you love to use? What makes you a unique leader? Knowing where you shine allows you to lead from a place of confidence and contribution rather than comparison.

Identifying career goals: What do you want from life? What legacy would you wish to give? What impact do you want to have on your team, organization, and world? The answers to these questions shape the roadmap to a career that doesn't just fill your schedule but fulfills your life.

Values and Goals

We discussed the importance of passion and purpose in leadership. Now, let's discuss how you bring these bad boys to life at work. Identifying your personal values and professional goals is crucial. Like peanut butter and jelly: two delicious flavours that go well! Values are the why, and goals are the what—when they're aligned, they create a rhythm in your leadership that others can follow instinctively.

Why bother aligning values and goals? Here's the deal:

Authenticity and Integrity:

Your actions are not a cloak of your values if they match your actions. You're leading like a boss, with authenticity and integrity. Your team and colleagues see that you're sincere and believe what you do. That builds trust and respect quicker than you can say promotion. And the best part? You don't have to pretend, posture, or overcompensate—people respond to leaders who are unapologetically aligned with their truth.

Fulfillment and Motivation:

We all want to feel like cogs in a machine. When your work reflects your values, you have not only clocked in and kicked out; you are making something that makes you feel fired up. And that, my friend, is the secret to staying motivated and fulfilled at work. This intrinsic motivation doesn't fade under pressure—it's the kind that stays lit even when the power goes out.

Resilience and Perseverance:

But once your values align with your goals, you have this inner strength, this never-giving-up attitude that helps you through the rough patches. It's like having an anti-trauma superpower. It doesn't make the hard times vanish, but it gives you a reason to push through them with grit and grace.

Decision-Making and Problem-Solving:

You are a superhero leader when your values drive your decisions. You make ethical, sustainable choices that support your long-term vision. Your team knows you have a moral compass, and they believe in your judgment. When the path isn't obvious, your principles become the map, and people will follow a leader who knows where they stand.

So, how do you actually align these values and goals? Here's the playbook:

1. Identify Your Core Values:

First things first: do some real soul-searching. What truly matters to you—not just on paper, but in the choices you make when no one's watching? What are your non-negotiables, the principles that guide your decisions and shape your character? These are your values and the inner compass of your leadership.

For example, maybe your core values include honesty, integrity, compassion, fairness, creativity, and innovation. These aren't just buzzwords; they're your personal mission statement for life—the blueprint of how you operate under pressure, how you treat others, and what you stand for when things get messy.

2. Define Your Professional Goals:

Who's on your career dream team? What kind of leader do you aspire to be—not someday, but starting now? What kind of legacy do you want to build for your team, your organization, or even the industry itself? Define your professional goals as clearly as you'd map out a road trip—you need a destination in mind before setting off. Example: Maybe your goal is to build an empowering, inclusive team culture. Or you're aiming to design revolutionary products, scale into global markets, or uplift your community through your business. Whatever it is, make it bold enough to excite you and clear enough to pursue.

3. Find the Overlap:

Now comes the magic—look for where your personal values intersect with your professional ambitions. Think of it as your own Venn diagram of awesomeness. That sweet spot is where your job becomes more than work—it becomes part of who you are.

For example, if you're driven by creativity and innovation and your goal is to launch game-changing products, boom—you've found your alignment. You're not just fulfilling a role; you're fuelling your purpose while delivering results. That's when your passion becomes contagious and your team starts moving in rhythm with your values.

4. Make Adjustments as Needed:

Let's face it—life doesn't stay still. As you evolve, so might your values and goals. If you wake up one day and realize you're climbing the wrong ladder, it's okay to pause, pivot, and redirect.

Maybe you value sustainability, but your company's carbon footprint makes you cringe. That's your cue. Either advocate for change internally or explore organizations that share your green ethos. Either way, you're making a conscious shift to realign with what matters to you. Don't be afraid to edit your journey. The draft isn't final until you say it is.

5. Communicate Your Values:

Don't keep your values locked in a journal, but share them. Let your team know what you stand for and why. This creates clarity and trust. It shows people the 'why' behind your decisions and helps them understand your leadership style.
Example: Mention your core values during onboarding chats, performance reviews, or team stand-ups. Say them out loud and show them in action. The more your team hears and sees your values, the more likely they are to mirror them.

6. Lead by Example:

Actions always speak louder than taglines. So don't just say you value respect, collaboration, or integrity—demonstrate it, even (and especially) when it's hard. Example: If you value integrity, stay transparent—even when the news isn't good. If collaboration is your thing, make sure meetings are inclusive and ideas are heard. Your behavior sets the tone for the entire team, and people take their cue from what you do far more than what you say.

7. Be Patient and Persistent:

Let's be real, this alignment thing isn't a quick hack. It takes reflection, self-awareness, and honest trial and error. But just like breaking in the perfect pair of boots, once it fits, you'll wonder how you ever worked without it. It's not about perfection. It's about progress, tuning in, adjusting, and showing up with more intention each day. And the payoff? A life that feels more like purpose and less like performance.

Finding Fulfillment and Creating a Positive Work Environment

So, let's talk about finding fulfillment at work and creating good vibes while you're at it. Sounds easier said than done, right? But it's not just some fluffy, feel-good ideal—it's a cornerstone of thriving teams and meaningful leadership.

It's about creating a space where people feel seen, valued, and excited to contribute. And when that happens, productivity isn't something you force; it's something that flows.

Now, how do you actually make that happen? Well, it's kind of like baking the perfect cake. You need the right ingredients, a bit of patience, and a willingness to try again if the first batch flops.

First off, you've got to fulfill yourself before you even think about inspiring others. Think about it: if you're dragging yourself out of bed each morning, dreading the day, how will you light a fire under anyone else? The secret to fulfillment? It's a bit like finding your favorite pair of jeans. You go through trial and error, trying things on, discarding what doesn't work—until suddenly, one day, it just fits. And when it fits, you know it. You feel it.

Ask yourself:

- What makes you feel alive at work?
- What tasks energize you rather than exhaust you?
- What environments bring out your best self?

Once you know what makes you tick, seek out or create opportunities that align with those motivators. That could mean taking on a new project, changing teams, or even building something of your own from the ground up. Just make sure it reflects the you that you're proud of.

Now, when it comes to creating a positive environment, this is where your leadership chops really show. Think of yourself as the conductor of an orchestra—you're not playing every instrument, but you're bringing harmony to the whole room.

Recognize your team's wins, both big and small. It doesn't take a fireworks display; sometimes, a simple thank-you or a shout-out in a meeting is all it takes to make someone feel seen. That kind of acknowledgment feeds morale in ways no bonus ever could.

Next up: communication. Keep it real and keep it open. Give your team a safe space to speak up—whether it's to share ideas, raise concerns, or admit a misstep. When people know they'll be heard and not judged, they'll take more initiative, own more responsibility, and collaborate more freely.

And let's not forget those values we talked about earlier. They're not just internal—they should be the bedrock of how your team operates. Make your values visible. Lead with them. And over time, you'll see those same values echoed in the people around you.

Oh, and here's a big one: work-life balance. Encourage it. Model it. Protect it. Burnout is the fast lane to disengagement, and nothing kills culture faster than a team that's running on fumes. Recharge people and they'll bring fresh energy to the table.

And yeah, some days will suck. Deadlines pile up. Tempers flare. Things break. That's when your leadership really matters. Stay grounded. Invite collaboration. Keep the learning mindset alive. Remind your team that every setback is a lesson dressed in rough edges.

And be real. Show that you're human, too. When you admit mistakes, laugh at yourself, and share your challenges, you create a space where others feel safe doing the same. That's not weakness—it's connection. And connection breeds loyalty, creativity, and grit.

Remember, creating a positive environment is a process, not a checklist. It takes constant effort, consistency, and honest communication. But the reward? A team that's not just productive, but passionate, united, and proud to show up every day.

So, be that leader. The one who sparks passion, walks in purpose, and builds a culture where people feel they truly belong. That's not just good leadership—it's the kind that leaves a legacy.

Chapter 9
Rule 7: "Everyone Has an Obligation to Dissent if It Is Done Appropriately and Respectfully"

The Power of Diverse Perspectives

Everyone must dissent if it is done appropriately and respectfully.

This rule might seem counterintuitive in a hierarchical setting where following orders is the norm. However, accepting dissent, encouraging diversity of opinions, and constructive criticism are essential ingredients for good decision-making and leadership.

True leadership doesn't demand uniform agreement—it welcomes informed challenge because it understands that progress often begins where comfort ends.

And by rebellion, I do not mean chaos. It isn't about lowering authority or creating a culture of negativity. It's about accepting that no person, brilliant or experienced, has the answers.

Even the most seasoned leader operates with incomplete information, and it's only through the interplay of differing perspectives that clarity and depth emerge. Creating an environment where everyone can question assumptions, offer different viewpoints, and contribute to finding the best possible solutions is not just a virtue—it's a necessity.

Why is embracing diverse perspectives important?

1. Unlocking Innovation and Creativity

People who think differently, challenge assumptions, and offer alternative points of view create a world of possibilities for us.

It’s not just about novelty—it’s about developing ideas that are bolder, richer, and more resilient. Different perspectives fuel creativity and innovation and produce stronger, more rounded solutions. It's like having experts from different specialities sharing knowledge and experience, each layer adding depth to the whole.

Example:

Imagine a new marketing team developing a campaign. People with the same background and viewpoint on the team are more apt to have similar approaches and ideas. However, a team with different experiences and backgrounds in advertising, design, technology, and psychology will probably create more creative and innovative ideas. Each individual doesn’t just bring skills, they bring lenses. And together, they can spot what others would miss, crafting messages that resonate more widely and genuinely.

2. Mitigating Bias and Blind Spots

Biases and blind spots are ingrained assumptions and perspectives that impair our ability to see things clearly. They’re not always intentional but if they are left unchallenged, they can become invisible forces that distort decision-making. Rather than encouraging biases, blind spots and constructive criticism, we can encourage different perspectives and make better decisions by actively inviting alternative viewpoints into the room.

Example:

Say a leadership team is considering a new product launch. A team with similar backgrounds and experiences may overlook issues or risks that are clear to those with different perspectives.

A varied team encompassing marketing, sales, engineering, and customer support can identify possible dangers and devise mitigation methods. What seems like a minor oversight in one department may appear as a major liability to another; this cross-checking is how smart organizations protect themselves from failure.

3. Building Stronger Solutions

Constructive criticism, when offered respectfully and focused on improvement, can be valuable for refining ideas, strategies, and stronger solutions. It's not about tearing things down for the sake of it; it's about pressure-testing concepts so they emerge sharper and more refined. It involves challenging assumptions, finding weaknesses, and challenging each other to think creatively and critically.

Example:

Imagine a team creating a new software application. If no one is prepared to give constructive criticism, bugs or usability issues may get missed until it is too late. However, if the team values openness to feedback and constructive criticism, those issues can be identified early in development and addressed. The goal isn't perfection—it's progress. And progress thrives in an environment where pushback is welcome, not punished.

4. Fostering a Culture of Learning

To accept diverse views and criticism constructively creates a culture of learning and improvement. It turns every interaction into a potential lesson, every disagreement into a deeper understanding. It forces people to question assumptions, search for new knowledge, and improve. This creates a flexible and growth-oriented environment, where learning isn't an occasional event—it's a daily habit.

Example:
Imagine a team that routinely gets constructive feedback where everyone is comfortable expressing ideas and challenging each other's perspectives. This generates an environment where everybody learns, builds skills, and learns more. It's not just about professional development; it's about intellectual curiosity and emotional maturity becoming part of the workplace.

5. Strengthening Team Cohesion

Rather counterintuitive, perhaps encouraging dissent can actually increase team cohesion. When people feel heard and respected, even when they disagree, they begin to trust the group more deeply. Team members feel safe expressing opinions that differ from the majority, which builds trust and respect. That allows for more collaborative and inclusive environments where everyone is heard and, more importantly, valued.

Example:
Imagine a team where everyone is comfortable speaking out, whether that means disagreeing with the leader or challenging the status quo. This honest communication builds trust and respect amongst the team. Disagreement doesn't erode unity; it reinforces it, provided it's done respectfully. And when people feel they can speak their truth without fear of dismissal or backlash, they contribute more fully and with greater pride.

The Importance of Respectful Dissent

Here's the thing: dissent must now be expressed courteously and productively. Neither hurting people nor undermining authority is appropriate. It entails challenging ideas, presenting alternative viewpoints, and contributing to better outcomes. In other words, it's not about being difficult; it's about being deliberate, thoughtful, and willing to engage in the kind of disagreement that sharpens outcomes instead of fracturing relationships.

A few key principles for respectful dissent:

Focus on the issue and not the person:

Rather, address the idea or proposal, not the person who presented it. Avoid personal attacks or critiques that damage relationships or create a hostile environment. The moment dissent becomes personal, it ceases to be productive—it shuts down dialogue, raises walls, and diverts energy from the idea itself to emotional defense.

Give specific constructive feedback:

Instead of saying "I disagree," justify your dissent with reasons, alternative solutions, and suggestions. This moves the conversation along and leads to better results. By offering clear, thoughtful rationale, you shift from opposition to contribution—dissent becomes a stepping stone rather than a stumbling block.

Be open to hearing:

Dissent is an all-encompassing issue. Accept other perspectives even if they challenge your own. Accept a change of mind if you have compelling evidence or arguments.

If you want the right to speak your truth, be prepared to listen to someone else's, and if the data, logic, or insight they bring is stronger, then evolving your view isn't weakness; it's leadership in action.

Respect others:

Keep a respectful tone and manner. Even when disagreeing, maintain a respectful tone and demeanour. Don't interrupt, scream, or use aggressive body language. Also, remember the objective is finding the best solution rather than winning an argument. Civility isn't just etiquette instead, it's the foundation for trust. Because even in disagreement, mutual respect keeps the door open for progress.

Dissent in Action: When Disagreement Breeds Success

Okay, we talked about how valuable diverse perspectives and constructive criticism are. Let's get real with real-life examples of how dissent can work better than expected. Because sometimes, the best ideas come from questioning assumptions, from waiting a minute. These stories don't just show how dissent functions; they show why it matters when the stakes are at their highest.

The Challenger Space Shuttle Disaster

One of the most tragic examples of the power of dissent is the 1986 Challenger Space Shuttle disaster. Engineers have asked about the cold safety of the O-rings in the solid rocket boosters. However, management overruled their concerns and launched the shuttle on time. This was a disaster, dumping seven astronauts and ending the space program. That tragic episode shows just how critical it is to listen to dissenters, whether they challenge the mainstream opinion or cause unsettling delays. It's a chilling reminder that ignoring inconvenient voices isn't just risky—it can be catastrophic, especially when lives are on the line.

The Ford Pinto Fuel Tank

The fuel tank of the Pinto model ruptured and exploded in rear-end collisions in the 1970s after Ford engineers fixed a design flaw. Yet cost-benefit analyses by Ford management found it cheaper to settle lawsuits over accidents than to redesign the fuel tank. This decision led to many injuries and deaths, focusing on short-term profits instead of safety. This damaged Ford's reputation and caused expensive legal battles. This example shows how suppressing dissent can be dangerous and how financial considerations override ethical and human safety considerations.

When people are afraid to speak or worse, when leadership refuses to hear, it's not just the brand that takes a hit; it's the conscience of the organization itself.

The Miracle on the Hudson

In 2009, both US Airways Flight 1549 engines failed due to a flock of geese after takeoff. Captain Chesley "Sully" Sullenberger and First Officer Jeffrey Skiles had to decide: Try returning to the airport or ditching the plane in the Hudson River.

Though the first simulations suggested a return to the airport was possible, Sullenberger disagreed based on experience and intuition. He considered a water landing safer despite the dangers. His decision was the right one despite tremendous pressure and uncertainty. The emergency landing of all 155 passengers and crew was successful because Sullenberger led the charge and challenged the initial assessment. This example shows how experience and intuition matter even when they contradict conventional wisdom or computer simulations. Sometimes, leadership means trusting your gut, especially when your gut is backed by decades of expertise and a calm mind under pressure.

The Apple Macintosh

The early 1980s saw Apple develop the Macintosh, an alternative personal computer to IBM's dominance. However, the company had disagreements over the Macintosh design and features. The leader of the Macintosh team, Steve Jobs, wanted to make a usable and pleasing computer, even if this meant giving up some technical capabilities. Some engineers and executives who valued technical specifications over user experience resisted this approach. Jobs stuck by his vision and pushed the team to build a powerful, intuitive computer. This produced a revolutionary personal computer that established Apple as synonymous with innovation and design. This example demonstrates how a vision can change things and how dissenting from the status quo can help you achieve breakthrough results. It also reveals how meaningful dissent isn’t always about contradicting someone else—sometimes it’s about holding fast to an idea no one else can yet see.

My Own Experiences with Dissent

Personally, I've seen dissent work to effect change. I remember being called upon to question established security protocols and suggest alternatives that I felt were better for my clients.

In the corporate world, I've encouraged my teams to challenge me on ideas and perspectives and push back when I disagree with them.

This has delivered stronger solutions and strategies and a more collaborative and innovative work environment. It's not always comfortable, but I'd take an honest challenge over quiet compliance any day of the week. Because in those conversations, we do more than solve problems—we build trust, creativity, and mutual respect.

Key Takeaways

Such examples show that dissent challenges assumptions, points out blind spots, and creates innovation. If we build a culture of diversity and constructive criticism, we get better results, avoid costly mistakes, and build a more dynamic and adaptable organization. Ultimately, respectful dissent isn't about resistance—it's about responsibility. It's how bold ideas are born, how strong decisions are made, and how the best leaders grow stronger, together with their teams.

Cultivating a Culture of Open Communication and Respectful Dissent

So, we know that dissent is useful for decision-making and innovation. But how do you build a culture where people feel comfortable speaking out, challenging the status quo, and offering constructive criticism without fear of reprisal?

It takes time. That requires intentionality, consistent leadership, and the will to create a climate where open communication and respectful dissent are not only allowed but actively encouraged. It means building an environment where dialogue replaces silence, and thoughtful disagreement becomes a sign of strength, not disloyalty.

Here is the Roadmap to Guide You

1. Lead by Example

You create the culture within your team. You must model open communication and dissent for others if you want to encourage it. Make your decisions transparent, solicit feedback, and listen to other perspectives, even if they challenge your own. Demonstrating vulnerability in leadership—being open about your own missteps or learning curves—can also set a powerful precedent that says: "This is a space where growth matters more than ego."

Example:
Explain to the team why you chose this and its meaning. Invite teammates to give feedback and suggestions and be flexible about your approach. When others see that your opinion isn't fixed and your authority isn't threatened by new ideas, they feel safe to speak freely.

2. Create a Safe Space

Create an environment where people feel free to speak out without being judged or punished. It means hearing other perspectives, acknowledging their validity, and responding constructively even if you disagree. Psychological safety doesn't emerge by accident; it's shaped through the way leaders respond to difficult conversations, unpopular ideas, and emotional honesty.

Example:
When a team member expresses dissent, thank them for their contribution, acknowledge their viewpoint, and explain why you disagree. Be careful not to interrupt, dismiss their concerns, or make them feel their opinion is not valued. That moment of grace could determine whether they ever speak up again.

3. Establish Clear Communication Channels

Offer various communication channels for open dialogue and feedback. It might involve weekly or monthly team meetings, one-on-one check-ins, suggestion boxes, anonymous feedback forms, or online forums for sharing ideas and concerns. When people have options in how they express themselves, you're more likely to hear the honest, unfiltered truth.

Example:

Introduce a weekday "open door" policy, allowing team members to schedule time to address issues or concerns they may have. Create an online forum for employees to share ideas, suggestions, and constructive dialogue, especially for those who may be hesitant to speak up in person.

4. Encourage Constructive Feedback

Make feedback a tool for improvement, not an attack on yourself.

Make specific behaviours or actions a focus for team members rather than generalization or personal criticisms. Provide training in giving and receiving feedback, emphasizing respectful communication and solution-focused. People often want to be helpful but lack the framework for giving feedback in a way that feels safe or useful.

Example:

Give specific feedback instead of saying, "You are always late for meetings.": "You've been late for the last three team meetings. I noticed. How do these delays happen?" This opens a path to reflection and resolution instead of defense and denial.

5. Embrace Diverse Perspectives

Actively seek out different perspectives and encourage your team to do so.

It might be inviting guest speakers with different backgrounds, creating cross-functional teams, or inviting employees to conferences or workshops outside of their area of expertise. Diversity of thought is often the driver of breakthroughs, especially in environments where everyone feels safe to disagree.

Example:
In your project team, include people from different departments or with different skill sets. That plurality of thought may lead to better ideas and possibilities for solving problems, exposing blind spots that a homogeneous team might overlook.

6. Recognize and Reward Dissent

Mention and reward those who dare to dissent constructively.

That might include public recognition, promotion, or other incentives that show you value diverse perspectives and open communication. The courage to speak out should be encouraged, not just tolerated.

Example:
Implement an Innovation Award for people or teams questioning the status quo and proposing new ideas.

Highlight examples of successful dissent in company newsletters or internal communications to show that different perspectives are valuable and often the starting point of progress.

7. Address Unproductive Dissent

Dissent is acceptable, but so is disrespectful or unproductive behaviour. If someone from the team regularly interrupts meetings, attacks the team publicly, or otherwise undermines team morale, address the issue privately and lay down expectations for the person. Constructive dissent isn't a license for disruption; it's a responsibility to challenge with care.

Example:
If one team member constantly interrupts others or dominates conversations, have a private conversation about their behaviour and offer advice on how to communicate better on the team. Clear expectations create a culture where freedom is balanced by responsibility.

8. Continuously Evaluate and Improve

Regularly assess how your team communicates and find room for improvement.

Take surveys, hold focus groups, or ask team members for feedback to understand their perspectives and identify barriers to open communication or respectful dissent. Culture isn't a fixed asset; it requires frequent tuning.

Example:
Take an anonymous survey about the team's communication climate. Ask questions about how comfortable team members are sharing their opinions, whether they feel heard and respected, and what improvements they would like to see. Use the results not just to assess, but to act.

9. Celebrate Successes

When dissent produces positive outcomes, rejoice in those successes and the contributions of those who challenged the status quo.

This demonstrates that different perspectives are valuable and fosters continued open communication and constructive criticism. When dissent results in something better, honour the process, not just the result.

Example:
If your team successfully implements an idea that was initially rejected, publicly acknowledge those who championed it and the good it has done for your team or organization. Celebrate those who didn't just go with the flow but helped redirect it entirely.

Applying these strategies to build an open organization with respect for dissent and communication is the key to success.

You empower your team to deliver exceptional work, challenge assumptions, and come up with creative solutions that make progress happen. And in doing so, you build not just a stronger business, but a braver, more thoughtful community where every voice has the power to shape the future.

Chapter 10
Rule 8: "Being Told When You Have Done Something Wrong Is Part of Learning How to Do It Right"

Feedback and Continuous Learning

Personal and professional development requires feedback. It is our mirror—showing our strengths and weaknesses.

Even negative feedback is difficult to receive, but it is part of learning and growing. Constructive feedback reveals how we learn, adjust our behaviours and perform. And while it can sting in the moment, its purpose isn't to bruise the ego but to sharpen performance—to turn blind spots into focus areas and repetition into refinement.

Feedback: A Catalyst for Growth

Feedback involves learning. Whether it is good feedback or areas for improvement, it helps people see themselves from another perspective. For instance, receiving feedback from more experienced peers or opponents in martial arts or rugby can be transformative. Standing in a bar and analyzing how an opponent performed compared to you or debriefing after a hard martial arts sparring session reveals little things you may not have noticed. This honest reflection promotes growth by identifying what went wrong and how to fix it. In those quiet moments—off the pitch or outside the gym—the real insights often emerge, and that's when the learning becomes embedded.

Feedback also stops stagnation. Even seasoned professionals like trainers or leaders need feedback. One trainer who has delivered sessions to tens of thousands of people may feel they know their stuff, but one comment about an offensive phrase in a particular culture can immediately change behaviour. These moments show how feedback keeps us relevant and adaptive—whatever our experience is. Without this check-in from others, even the best of us can veer off course without realizing it, and the result isn't just outdated content—it's lost credibility.

The Challenge of Receiving Feedback

In reality, though, nobody particularly enjoys negative feedback. Though many claim they welcome honest input, criticism is often a psychological barrier. We tend to get defensive, deny the critique's validity, or push back. So, if I get feedback I dislike, I instinctively argue or dismiss it. However, I've learned to weigh its validity and often find it backed up by close friends or relatives. I either accept the feedback, make changes, acknowledge it and move on. But make no mistake, that doesn't happen in a single breath—it happens in the silence that follows, in the self-talk that sorts through pride, logic, and the quiet truth we often resist.

That internal process of wrestling with feedback is critical. They teach us resilience and emotional intelligence for leadership and personal development. Learn to separate emotion from the message so we can pay attention to the value feedback brings instead of our immediate reactions. The quicker we learn to hear without flinching, the quicker we grow—not just professionally, but as people others want to follow.

Continuous Learning through Feedback

The feedback drives continuous learning by closing the gap between where we are and where we want to be. And it ensures that our growth is not random but guided by deliberate insights. This is most evident in professional sports development. Coaches and teammates frequently give athletes direct, sometimes harsh feedback. This feedback is hard to hear but shapes their skills and strategies for improved performance. Each session, each drill, becomes part of an evolving feedback loop—tightening focus, recalibrating goals, and transforming raw potential into polished execution.

Performance evaluations and peer reviews also help employees align their contributions with company goals. However, one troubling trend in modern workplaces is that some people cannot take criticism. Feedback is perceived instead as a threat to capabilities rather than an opportunity for growth. Such a mindset kills the purpose of feedback and kills personal development. And more worryingly, it creates a defensive work culture where progress halts—not because ideas run dry, but because egos refuse to evolve.

Role of Feedback in Leadership

Feedback is doubly important for leaders. Firstly, feedback helps leaders refine their decision-making and communication skills. Secondly, giving feedback is part of leadership. Leaders who encourage honest communication in their teams promote learning. In teams where feedback flows upward and downward, accountability doesn't feel imposed—it feels shared, and that's what drives performance from within.

A growth mindset leader—someone who believes abilities develop with practice and hard work—will seek feedback for themselves and encourage team members to do the same. In this way, mistakes become steps to success instead of failures in the workplace. Leaders encourage experimentation and constructive feedback to help teams learn from failures and innovate. Because without feedback, leadership becomes guesswork—and with it, it becomes guidance rooted in awareness.

Strategies for Embracing Feedback

1. Active Listening:

Receive feedback by focusing on understanding the message rather than preparing a defence. Listening attentively and respectfully not only shows that you value the person giving the feedback, but it also ensures that you're capturing the full nuance of their perspective, especially when the topic touches on sensitive or critical areas of performance.

2. **Seek Specificity:**

Negative general feedback like "You need to improve" is useless. Ask for examples and concrete suggestions instead. By prompting specificity, you shift the conversation from vague opinion to actionable insight, allowing for real learning and measurable progress.

3. **Avoid Emotional Reactivity:**

Defensive feelings are natural—just be objective about the feedback. Consider it carefully before responding. Take time to pause and reflect. Reacting emotionally can cloud judgment, but pausing allows reason and growth to take precedence over pride or ego.

4. **Validate Feedback:**

Seek additional opinions about whether the feedback echoes other observations. This lets you know if you should act on it. Corroborating feedback with multiple sources helps distinguish isolated comments from consistent patterns that genuinely require attention.

5. **Create Feedback Loops:**

Frequently ask peers, supervisors, and mentors for feedback. Continuous input identifies patterns and tracks your progress. A feedback loop builds a rhythm of improvement, where each round of input serves as a checkpoint rather than a judgment—encouraging refinement, not retribution.

The Greater Impact of Feedback

Feedback has a ripple effect if embraced. The openness of a leader to feedback motivates the team to follow suit. This creates an organizational culture of learning and innovation. In turn, avoiding feedback or denying it creates complacency and stagnation. The tone set by leadership becomes the baseline for team behavior—when leaders treat feedback as a gift, not a threat, it encourages everyone to pursue excellence rather than settle for adequacy.

Strategies for Providing and Receiving Constructive Feedback

Providing feedback is essential for personal and professional development. Learning to provide and receive constructive feedback can enhance performance and relationships in leadership, education, and other fields. Mastering this skill not only sharpens the growth of others but demonstrates maturity, empathy, and foresight in the one delivering it.

Strategies for Providing Constructive Feedback

1. **Start with Positive Intentions:**

Feedback should promote growth, not criticize or denigrate. Provide feedback that reflects genuine care and concern. This approach lets the individual receiving feedback feel supported and not attacked, reinforcing that the goal is collaboration, not correction for its own sake.

2. **Be Specific and Objective:**

General remarks like "You should do better" are unhelpful. Instead, focus on instances of behaviour or performance to improve. Instead of saying, "Your presentation was bad," you may add, "Your presentation lacked examples to support the points." This specificity provides actionable insights, reducing ambiguity and increasing the likelihood of improvement.

3. **Try the "Feedback Sandwich" Technique:**

Begin with positive feedback, then focus on areas for growth, and conclude with encouragement. For example: "Your energy at the meeting was amazing and kept everyone engaged. I wish the info you supplied was more detailed. Better preparation can enhance the impact of your presentations." The sandwich technique softens the delivery without watering down the message, making it more digestible and less emotionally jarring.

4. **Provide Timely Feedback:**

Feedback should be provided as soon as possible after the event or behaviour. Delayed input may be irrelevant or inconsequential, and the individual may not recall the experience accurately. Timeliness ensures clarity, preserves context, and boosts the chance that lessons will be retained and applied.

5. Emphasize Behaviours, Not Personalities:

When offering comments, focus on concrete acts rather than personal traits. You may have stated, "Your approach to that client issue was more empathetic," rather than "You're not an excellent empathetic person." Maintaining this separation helps prevent defensiveness and keeps the conversation anchored in professionalism rather than personal critique.

6. Encourage Two-Way Conversation:

Constructive feedback involves two-way communication. Allow recipients to express their perspectives and ask questions. This discourse promotes understanding and clarity of objectives and shows that you value dialogue over monologue—fostering a more balanced and respectful exchange.

7. Tailor Your Feedback Approach:

Individuals react to feedback differently. Some individuals like direct communication, while others prefer a more indirect method. Adjust your tone and delivery to the recipient's personality and preferences. A flexible approach increases receptiveness and minimizes resistance, allowing the message to land more effectively.

8. Highlight the Path Forward:

Feedback should address mistakes and suggest ways to improve. To address a skill gap, offer resources, mentoring, or training. Framing feedback within a forward-looking context transforms it from a critique into a roadmap—one that leads not just to correction, but to competence and confidence.

Strategies for Receiving Constructive Feedback

1. Have a Growth Mindset:

First, get rid of that fixed mindset where you either are good at this or you aren't—embrace the growth mindset, the belief that you can always improve, grow, and become better with effort, reflection, and persistence. Consider both positive and negative feedback as a gift—a unique chance to uncover blind spots, develop new skills, and sharpen your overall awareness.

Imagine learning to ride a bicycle. You're wobbling at first; maybe you spill a few beers. But you get the hang of it with practice, perseverance—and perhaps a few words from someone who understands the two-wheeled balance act. Feedback is like that friend who helps you adjust your grip, recalibrate your center of gravity, and eventually glide down the road with control and confidence.

2. Listen Without Interrupting:

When someone gives you feedback—especially critical input—your instinct might be to jump in, explain yourself, or defend your choices. But resist that urge. Breathe deeply, listen fully, and allow them to finish before you respond. This not only shows basic respect but also gives you a chance to truly understand their point of view, process the information, and respond in a thoughtful, composed manner.

Imagine this: you're in a meaningful conversation. If you interrupt, jump to conclusions, or hijack the dialogue, the other person will feel unheard and invalidated. It's the same with feedback—if you give them space to speak, you'll grasp more of their message and can engage with it in a way that fosters growth, not conflict.

3. Detach Emotions from Feedback:

Nobody likes hearing they messed up or could do better. It's natural to feel hurt, defensive, or even irritated. But the key is learning to detach your emotional reaction from the message itself.

Focus on the content of the feedback—not the tone, not the person delivering it, and not your immediate emotional response. Feedback is about your actions or choices, not your worth or character.

Imagine you're a chef, and a respected food critic gives a poor review of your signature dish. It stings, of course—but rather than seeing it as a personal attack, you could use their insights to tweak your recipe, refine your seasoning, or explore a better plating technique. That's how feedback works—it gives you a roadmap for improvement, not a verdict on your value.

4. Clarify and Ask Questions:

Feedback can sometimes be vague or incomplete. If the message isn't clear or actionable, don't shy away from asking questions or requesting specific examples.

This signals that you're serious about improvement and eager to understand what changes are needed—not just nodding politely to move on.

Imagine you're a student and your teacher scribbles, "Needs more depth" on your essay. You wouldn't just accept that without knowing where or how to add depth. You'd ask what sections need elaboration or what concepts were too shallow. Treat feedback at work the same way—ask for clarity, and the quality of your response will improve dramatically.

5. Reflect:

Okay, so you've received some feedback—maybe even the kind that makes your stomach twist. Don't react impulsively. Take a moment, inhale deeply, and allow yourself the space to process before you respond or make decisions.

Reflection, like a post-workout cooldown, lets you review the message with objectivity and plan your next step with clarity and focus.

Imagine taking a hit in a boxing ring. Your first impulse might be to strike back or crumble, but a seasoned fighter takes a beat—assesses the damage, recalibrates the stance, and plans the next move. Feedback requires the same internal discipline: acknowledge the sting, then get strategic.

6. Acknowledge and Appreciate Feedback:

Whether or not you agree with what's been said, acknowledge the feedback and express appreciation. A simple "thank you" shows maturity, openness, and a willingness to engage in meaningful dialogue. It also encourages continued communication, setting the tone for ongoing growth and partnership.

Picture yourself as an artist unveiling your work. Even if a viewer's critique doesn't align with your vision, recognizing their perspective and thanking them preserves the creative exchange. Similarly, showing appreciation in a professional setting builds rapport and trust—and keeps the door open for future feedback.

7. Validate Feedback from Established Sources:

Not all feedback will be accurate, fair, or given with the right intentions. If something feels off, get a second opinion. Turn to someone who knows your work, understands your character, and can provide an honest, informed perspective. This helps you assess the feedback's legitimacy and decide whether action is necessary—or whether it's best left behind.

Picture this: you're a doctor faced with a complex case. You wouldn't rely solely on your instinct—you'd consult colleagues, review the data, and possibly refer the patient for a second opinion. The same logic applies to professional feedback—validate before internalizing.

8. Develop an Action Plan:

Feedback becomes powerful when it inspires meaningful action. Once you've understood the input, translate it into a practical plan: set measurable, relevant, and time-bound goals that reflect the suggested improvements.

Identify the support or resources you'll need—whether it's mentorship, new training, or peer collaboration—and track your progress with intention.

Imagine you're training for a marathon. You don't just lace up your shoes and start running—you create a structured plan, monitor your mileage, adapt your routines based on performance, and adjust with each coach's tip. The same approach works in professional life: turn feedback into fuel by using it to build a tangible, purposeful path forward.

Tips for Using Feedback to Improve Performance

1. Track Feedback Over Time:

Monitor feedback patterns to discover recurring themes and persistent blind spots. This ongoing record can help you focus your efforts, identify areas needing the most attention, and measure your progress in tangible, meaningful ways.

2. Act on Feedback Promptly:

Don't let valuable feedback collect dust. Implement changes as soon as possible to demonstrate your commitment to growth and show others that you take their insights seriously.

3. Seek Feedback Proactively:

Don't wait for a yearly review or a formal assessment. Cultivate the habit of regularly seeking feedback from mentors, colleagues, or supervisors. This positions you ahead of potential issues and keeps your development trajectory aligned with evolving goals.

4. Balance Feedback with Self-Reflection:

External feedback is essential, but it should be paired with internal reflection. Regularly assess your own performance with a critical yet compassionate eye, recognizing patterns before they become problems.

5. Celebrate Progress and Success:

When you implement feedback and see real results—whether it's improved communication, stronger leadership, or greater efficiency—take a moment to acknowledge your achievement. Celebrating small wins strengthens your motivation to keep improving.

6. Build a Feedback-Friendly Culture:

In any team or organization, normalize feedback as a vital

part of development. Encourage peer reviews, anonymous suggestions, and regular check-ins to ensure that feedback flows openly and constructively at all levels.

7. Understand the Context of Feedback:

Not all feedback is created equal. Consider the context—who it came from, their intent, and the environment in which it was given. Cultural differences, emotional states, and hierarchical dynamics can all color the way feedback is communicated and received.

8. Use Feedback as a Learning Opportunity:

Regardless of tone or timing, feedback has the potential to teach something valuable—if approached with the right mindset. Treat it as a guide to new skills, deeper awareness, and better habits, even if it's uncomfortable at first.

Importance of Feedback in Leadership

Leaders must not only give feedback but also model how to receive it gracefully. Those who offer clear, actionable, and timely insights enable their teams to improve, and those who remain open to critique reveal a humility that fosters trust and loyalty.

While giving or receiving feedback may feel awkward or even painful at times, the benefits far outweigh the momentary discomfort. By applying the strategies outlined here, both individuals and leaders can use feedback as a powerful vehicle for growth and transformation.

Practical Tips for Using Feedback to Improve Performance and Grow as a Leader

Let's now focus on execution. Because feedback, no matter how brilliant or insightful, means very little if it's not acted upon. It's like receiving a treasure map but never setting off to find the gold.

The truth is, feedback—no matter how abrasive or difficult to swallow—is an opportunity. A chance to challenge your assumptions, explore your blind spots, and discover where your strengths have room to expand.

You may be thinking, "Easier said than done," especially when that feedback cuts into your sense of self. But with the right perspective and a thoughtful plan, those sharp words can become stepping stones to powerful leadership.

1. Accept the Power of Reflection:

Before you leap into action, take a moment to digest the feedback you've received. Don't brush it aside or label it irrelevant. Ask yourself what themes are emerging, what patterns are repeating, and where your attention is most needed.

Imagine yourself as a detective reviewing a complex case. You wouldn't arrest a suspect based on one clue—you'd gather evidence, form hypotheses, and approach the situation methodically. Feedback works the same way. Analyze it before acting.

2. Set SMART Goals:

Once you've clarified the areas for growth, set SMART goals—Specific, Measurable, Achievable, Relevant, and Time-bound. Don't just say, "I need to improve communication." Say, "I will enhance my listening skills by completing a communication workshop within four weeks."

Picture yourself as a pilot preparing for a flight. You wouldn't take off without a flight plan. You'd chart the route, monitor the weather, adjust altitude, and track your progress to ensure a smooth landing. Goal setting does the same for your leadership development.

3. Ask for Help and Resources:

You're not expected to figure it all out alone. Reach out to colleagues, coaches, or mentors who can offer guidance and share relevant tools—whether it's a course, a book, or just honest advice.

Think of yourself as a chef experimenting with a new technique. You wouldn't just wing it and hope for the best. You'd consult cookbooks, ask experienced chefs, or take a class to refine your craft. Leadership is no different—ask, learn, and grow.

4. Practice Deliberately:

Leadership, like any skill, gets better with consistent practice. Don't expect transformation overnight.

Improvement is gradual and comes from sustained effort, reflection, and repetition.

Picture yourself as a violinist mastering a difficult piece. You wouldn't expect brilliance after one practice session. You'd tune your instrument, rehearse the same passage dozens of times, and refine your technique with every stroke. Leadership requires the same commitment.

5. Celebrate Your Progress:

Recognize your wins, even the small ones. When you apply feedback and achieve a milestone—whether it's managing a tough conversation with grace or leading a project more effectively—celebrate that progress.

Imagine climbing a mountain. You don't wait until the summit to pause and admire the view. You stop at each ridge, mark your progress, and draw energy from how far you've come. Feedback should energize you, not just instruct you.

6. Embrace the Feedback Loop:

Don't treat feedback as a one-time event. Make it a continuous cycle—receive input, reflect, adapt, and seek more. Embed it into your routine as a vital part of personal and professional development.

Think of yourself as a gardener tending to a vibrant garden. You don't just plant the seeds and walk away. You water, prune, watch how things grow, and adjust your approach with the seasons. Growth is sustained by attention and feedback.

Chapter 11
Rule 9: "A Person's View Is Always Based on the Information They Have. So They Are Not Wrong, They Just Have Incomplete Information"

The Essence of Informed Decision-Making: Navigating Complexity with Clarity

At the heart of effective leadership lies a deep truth: a person's view is fundamentally shaped by the information they possess. Thus, they are not inherently "wrong," but rather operating from a place of limited or incomplete understanding. Rule 9 underscores the vital importance of grounding decisions in solid, comprehensive information. While empathy and communication remain critical leadership traits, they serve not as ends in themselves, but as conduits to more informed, balanced, and deliberate decision-making.

In the face of complex decisions, leaders must actively seek out a plurality of perspectives. This requires more than just passive listening; it demands a deliberate commitment to surfacing dissenting views, uncovering blind spots, and opening up space for honest feedback. As emphasized in Rule 7, "Everyone has an obligation to dissent." It is within the friction of competing views that sharper insights often emerge, leading to decisions that are not only wiser, but also more resilient.

In our rapidly evolving world, where data flows in torrents and the pace of change is unrelenting, leaders now have access to sophisticated tools like artificial intelligence and predictive analytics. Yet, these instruments, however advanced, are only as effective as the discernment and humility of those who use them. Relying solely on one's interpretation of data can lead to biased conclusions. Instead, leaders should cultivate a habit of questioning their assumptions and inviting diverse viewpoints into the decision-making process.

The Role of Diverse Perspectives in Decision-Making

1. The Importance of Information Gathering

Decision-making should never be an isolated act. It is a collaborative effort that requires drawing from diverse sources, internal and external, quantitative and qualitative, strategic and intuitive. Leaders must engage widely, listen intently, and gather insight through formal channels as well as informal conversations. Each perspective adds dimension, helping to reduce blind spots and enrich understanding.

Example: Consider a situation where a leader must decide on a new product launch. Instead of relying solely on their instincts, they incorporate feedback from market research, customer service trends, and internal brainstorming sessions. This mirrors Apple's approach when preparing to launch the iPhone: a painstaking synthesis of consumer behavior, evolving tech landscapes, and user expectations. The result was not just a product rather it was a shift in culture. Moreover, that was possible because decisions weren't made in isolation, but in the crucible of collective insight.

2. Embracing Different Opinions

Engaging with differing views isn't just a democratic gesture but a strategic necessity. Dissent, when encouraged in a respectful and curious environment, becomes a tool for surfacing hidden truths and sharpening judgment. The aim is not to reach consensus, but to explore complexity and uncover layers that may have otherwise gone unnoticed.

Example: Picture a team debating two opposing approaches to a client project. Rather than dismiss the minority opinion, a wise leader opens the floor to a constructive back-and-forth. In the world of personal protection, for instance, security teams often differ on tactical routes. By allowing all options to be heard and debated, they reduce risk and expand preparedness. The same logic applies in boardrooms: dissent illuminates what silence conceals, ultimately enabling stronger, more defensible decisions.

3. The Challenge of Personal Bias

Bias is a constant shadow in decision-making. It emerges not only from personal experiences, but also from education, culture, and past failures or victories. Good leaders don't eliminate bias but acknowledge it, examine it, and counterbalance it through feedback and diversity of thought.

Example: A marketing executive who has long favored print campaigns may instinctively shy away from social media. However, by listening to a younger team member versed in digital trends, they open a door to innovation. This scenario echoes Kodak's fatal reluctance to embrace digital photography, which is a blind spot that proved catastrophic. In contrast, Netflix succeeded by discarding assumptions and adapting early, driven by curiosity and an openness to challenge its own business model.

4. Leveraging Technology for Better Decision-Making

Data without context is just noise. And while technology can process staggering volumes of data at breathtaking speeds, it cannot feel nuance, interpret tone, or weigh moral consequence. These remain human responsibilities. Technology should enhance decisions and not be considered a substitute for the human faculty of judgment.

Example: A retail brand uses AI to analyze customer reviews and purchasing patterns. The machine flags declining interest in a particular product line, but it's the team that is armed with market experience and consumer insight that interprets what the data means and how to respond. During the COVID-19 pandemic, data became essential in guiding shifts in consumer behavior. Restaurants, for instance, adjusted delivery menus and redesigned online experiences in real time which is driven by analytics, but executed with empathy and human oversight.

5. The Fluidity of Decisions

Leadership requires adaptability. A decision is not a verdict but a response to the best available information at a given time. But new facts emerge, environments shift, and assumptions unravel. The strongest leaders are those who can pivot without shame or ego, adjusting course when clarity improves.

Example: After launching a digital product, a leader notices unexpected user behaviors. Instead of defending the original blueprint, they regroup, consult new data, and implement a swift update. This nimbleness reflects mastery. The automotive industry's pivot toward electric vehicles is a case in point—manufacturers like Ford and GM have reoriented strategies not out of panic, but from reading the signs and choosing to evolve before being forced to. Changing one's mind, in this light, is not a weakness. It's a discipline.

Good leadership does not come from rigid certainty but it comes from a humble willingness to evolve. The best decisions are made not in isolation, but in conversation. They are not made once, but remade as needed, fueled by a continuous stream of feedback, challenge, and curiosity.

Ultimately, the essence of Rule 9 is: people aren't always wrong, they just don't know what they don't know.

The responsibility of a leader is to uncover what's missing, to invite others into that search, and to remain open enough to grow as the picture becomes clearer.

The Power of the Wheel Metaphor

One of my former bosses once provided me with a powerful analogy that stayed with me: he linked his leadership style to the hub of a wheel, with his team as the spokes. If all the spokes are on one side, the wheel will collapse the moment it turns. However, if the spokes are evenly distributed, the wheel can spin with purpose and stability. His leadership approach mirrored that of the wheel: he brought together people with different attitudes, risk appetites, technical skills, and lived experiences. His role, as the hub, was to listen, synthesize, and decide—not based on his perspective alone, but on the collective wisdom of the group.

This metaphor illustrates the importance of diverse perspectives in the decision-making process. Each spoke, representing a unique viewpoint, contributes to the overall strength and functionality of the wheel. A wheel turns smoothly only when each spoke plays its part in maintaining balance and structure. Similarly, when leaders embrace a diversity of thought—technical, emotional, cultural, and strategic—they foster a team dynamic that is both resilient and responsive.

Encouraging input from across the organization is not merely a courtesy—it is a strategic imperative. The more perspectives a leader draws upon, the broader the field of vision becomes. In times of uncertainty or rapid change, this multifaceted awareness becomes essential. Leaders who consciously construct their "wheel" with a rich variety of spokes are better equipped to pivot, accelerate, or endure the inevitable bumps in the road.

Listening to Understand: The Art of Active Engagement

Listening is often misunderstood as a passive activity; however, effective listening is an active, intentional discipline—one that is essential for strong leadership. Many individuals listen with the intent to respond, rather than to understand. This reflexive approach can hinder communication and create a false sense of alignment, ultimately leading to confusion, misinterpretation, or disengagement. To foster a culture of informed decision-making, leaders must master the art of listening not just to what is said, but to why it is said and sometimes, to what remains unsaid.

1. Active Listening vs. Waiting to Speak

Active listening requires attention, focus, and engagement. It involves not just hearing the words being spoken, but also tuning into the emotions, motivations, and context behind them. Leaders who practice this form of listening create a space where team members feel heard, respected, and genuinely valued. It sets a tone that elevates conversation from transactional to transformational.

Example: In a high-stakes negotiation, a skilled negotiator will listen intently to the other party's concerns and objectives, rather than merely waiting for their turn to speak. This active engagement fosters mutual respect and can lead to a deeper understanding of the other party's motivations, ultimately paving the way for a more thoughtful and mutually beneficial agreement. When leaders model this type of listening, they send a message: "Your voice matters. Your insight counts."

2. The Importance of Nonverbal Communication

Communication extends well beyond spoken words. Nonverbal cues like body language, tone of voice, eye contact, and facial expressions often reveal truths that language may mask or dilute. Leaders who are attuned to these subtle signals are better able to assess team morale, gauge emotional undercurrents, and respond with precision.

Example: During a team meeting, a leader may notice that one team member appears disengaged or uneasy. Rather than overlook it, the observant leader may take the time to check in privately, offering space for that person to express concerns or frustrations. This kind of attention demonstrates not only emotional intelligence but also proactive care. It's in these quiet moments of recognition that trust is built and inclusion deepened.

When leaders fail to notice—or worse, ignore—nonverbal feedback, they risk missing vital signals that could help them course-correct or intervene early. Effective communication requires not only speaking clearly but seeing attentively.

3. Creating Psychological Safety

For team members to speak up, leaders must cultivate an environment where candor is welcomed, not punished. Psychological safety—the belief that one can share ideas, concerns, or mistakes without fear of humiliation or retaliation—is the foundation for open dialogue and innovation.

Example: Google's Project Aristotle, a multi-year study exploring team effectiveness, identified psychological safety as the most critical factor in high-performing teams. Teams that felt safe to express their thoughts and admit uncertainty were more collaborative, resilient, and creative. By modeling vulnerability, asking thoughtful questions, and rewarding curiosity over conformity, leaders foster an environment where informed dissent becomes a norm and where risks are taken in service of progress.

In psychologically safe teams, disagreement isn't a threat—it's a tool for refining ideas and sharpening collective intelligence.

4. Empathy in Listening

Empathy, the ability to place oneself in another's shoes, is not just an emotional competency but it's a strategic one. When leaders listen with empathy, they aren't simply absorbing data; they are connecting with the deeper human dimensions that drive performance, engagement, and loyalty.

Example: A manager may notice that a typically high-performing employee has become withdrawn. Rather than reprimanding the drop in productivity, the manager checks in privately and listens with patience and compassion. Perhaps the team member is facing personal struggles or health concerns. By creating space for honesty, the leader not only offers meaningful support but also earns trust that will echo beyond that single exchange.

Empathy doesn't mean avoiding tough decisions; it means approaching them with context. It means tempering firmness with grace and remembering that behind every KPI is a human being with a story.

This empathetic response fosters a sense of belonging and loyalty, ultimately leading to a more engaged and motivated team.

Effective Communication: The Bridge to Understanding

Effective communication is essential for conveying ideas, sharing information, and fostering collaboration within a team. It is the connective tissue that binds vision to execution and transforms individual contributors into a cohesive unit. Leaders must prioritize clear and respectful communication to ensure that messages are understood, misinterpretations are minimized, and that team members feel seen, heard, and valued.

When communication flows well, trust deepens, and clarity takes the place of confusion. It is not just about transmitting information—it's about shaping meaning, building relationships, and guiding collective effort toward a common goal.

1. Clarity in Messaging

Leaders must communicate their expectations, goals, and vision with clarity. Ambiguous or vague messaging can lead to confusion, misalignment, and missed deadlines. In contrast, clear direction enables individuals to understand not only *what* needs to be done, but *why* it matters.

Example: A leader outlining a new project should provide specific details regarding objectives, timelines, and roles. By clearly articulating these elements, the leader ensures that everyone understands their responsibilities and the overall direction of the project. This eliminates the need for second-guessing and empowers the team to act with confidence and purpose.

In high-stakes situations or periods of change, clarity becomes even more crucial. The more unpredictable the terrain, the more essential it is for a leader to serve as a steady guide—one whose words clarify the path forward rather than obscure it.

2. Encouraging Open Dialogue

Effective communication involves creating opportunities for open dialogue. Leaders should not simply deliver directives but should actively engage in two-way conversations, where questions are welcomed, and differing perspectives are not just tolerated but encouraged.

Example: During a team meeting, a leader may pose open-ended questions to prompt discussion, such as, "What challenges do you foresee in this project, and how can we address them together?" This approach invites collaboration and demonstrates the leader's commitment to valuing diverse perspectives.

Open dialogue is more than a strategy—it's a signal. It shows that the leader is not just instructing, but listening; not just speaking, but learning. Over time, this builds a culture of psychological safety, where individuals know their contributions matter and are more willing to surface difficult truths or fresh insights.

3. Respectful Communication

Respectful communication is vital for fostering positive relationships within a team. Leaders must be mindful of their tone, language, and approach, ensuring that they convey messages with kindness and consideration, even when addressing conflict or giving critical feedback.

Example: When providing feedback, a leader should focus on constructive criticism rather than personal attacks. By framing feedback in a respectful manner, the leader encourages growth and development while maintaining a positive team dynamic.

Respect is not a soft skill; it's a structural one. It creates the conditions under which trust can grow, innovation can thrive, and disagreement can be productive rather than personal. A respectful leader sets the emotional tone of the workplace—where dignity is non-negotiable, even in the midst of challenge.

4. Utilising Technology for Communication

In today's digital age, technology plays a significant role in communication. Leaders must be proactive in leveraging various communication tools to facilitate real-time collaboration, especially in increasingly remote or hybrid work environments.

Example: Utilizing platforms like Slack or Microsoft Teams can enhance real-time communication among team members. Leaders can create channels for specific projects or topics, allowing for organized discussions and information sharing. This approach fosters a sense of connection and collaboration, even when team members are physically apart.

Yet, the use of technology must be intentional. Over-reliance on digital tools without clarity of purpose can lead to information overload, fragmented conversations, and disengagement. Leaders should model effective digital etiquette, striking a balance between connectivity and cognitive space.

5. The Role of Storytelling

Storytelling is a powerful communication tool that can enhance understanding, build emotional resonance, and sustain engagement. Stories go beyond facts—they humanize data, contextualize decisions, and infuse meaning into everyday tasks.

Example: A leader may share a personal story about a challenging decision they faced and the lessons learned from that experience. This storytelling approach not only humanizes the leader but also provides valuable insights that resonate with team members.

When leaders tell stories—of failure, resilience, success, or doubt—they create a bridge between authority and authenticity. Stories invite listeners in. They don't just inform; they inspire. In a world saturated with metrics, storytelling reminds us that leadership is, at its core, a deeply human endeavor.

The Consequences of Incomplete Information: Lessons from the Past

To understand the critical importance of informed decision-making, it is beneficial to examine real-world scenarios where decisions, made in the absence of complete or accurate information, led to far-reaching and often disastrous consequences. These cautionary tales serve not merely as historical footnotes but as enduring reminders that leaders must actively seek comprehensive insight before committing to a course of action—and that agility in the face of evolving information is often the difference between success and failure.

Each example that follows underscores a key principle: the quality of any decision is directly correlated to the breadth, depth, and diversity of information available at the time it is made.

1. The 3G License Auction: A Cautionary Tale in Technological Overconfidence

In the early 2000s, telecom operators across Europe participated in high-stakes auctions for 3G licenses, spending astronomical sums to secure the right to provide next-generation mobile services. Industry giants such as Deutsche Telekom and Vodafone invested heavily, buoyed by the prevailing belief that 3G technology would usher in a telecommunications revolution and yield substantial returns.

However, this optimism proved premature. As the market evolved and consumer behavior shifted, the anticipated adoption rates lagged behind expectations. Soon after the rollout of 3G, the next wave—4G—emerged with even greater promise, rendering previous investments less impactful. The substantial financial commitments made for 3G licenses became sunk costs that failed to yield proportionate value, forcing many companies to write off large portions of their investments.

This episode underscores a critical leadership failure: the inability to anticipate rapid technological evolution and shifts in consumer demand. Leaders were so focused on securing market share that they neglected to question the long-term viability of the technology in light of emerging trends. Their decisions, rooted in narrow or outdated assumptions, became liabilities.

2. Kodak's Downfall: When Legacy Becomes a Limitation

Kodak's decline is often cited as a textbook example of a company brought down by its own legacy. Once an undisputed leader in photography, Kodak ironically pioneered digital photography in the 1970s but failed to capitalize on its own innovation. The leadership team, anchored to the profitability of traditional film products, underestimated the magnitude of the digital shift and clung to a business model that was rapidly becoming obsolete.

As digital photography gained momentum, Kodak's reluctance to pivot proved fatal. By the time the company made earnest attempts to transition, it had lost its competitive edge. In 2012, Kodak filed for bankruptcy, unable to recover from years of strategic inertia.

Kodak's story is more than a tale of technological disruption—it is a sobering example of what happens when leaders base decisions on outdated information and resist updating their worldview. It highlights the perils of failing to challenge entrenched assumptions and the importance of continually reassessing the market landscape.

3. Blockbuster's Missed Opportunities: The Cost of Ignoring Signals

Blockbuster, once a titan in the video rental industry, offers another instructive example. As consumer preferences began to shift toward on-demand digital content, companies like Netflix began experimenting with mail-order DVDs and eventually online streaming. Blockbuster, by contrast, remained anchored to its brick-and-mortar model, dismissing the emerging threat posed by digital platforms.

Despite having multiple opportunities to acquire Netflix in its early stages, Blockbuster's leadership declined, viewing the streaming model as peripheral rather than transformational. This misjudgment proved fatal. By the time Blockbuster recognized the magnitude of the digital shift, it was too late to catch up. In 2010, the company filed for bankruptcy, a victim of its own unwillingness to adapt.

Blockbuster's fall is a vivid example of the danger of strategic tunnel vision—when decision-makers fail to interpret market signals and evolving customer behavior. It demonstrates that clinging to the familiar can be far riskier than venturing into the unknown.

4. Military Operations and Intelligence Failures: The High Price of Uncertainty

In military operations, the consequences of incomplete or inaccurate information are often measured not in financial losses but in human lives. Intelligence, when flawed or fragmented, can compromise even the most well-planned missions.

Example 1: Operation Neptune Spear (2010) In 2010, U.S. Navy SEALs executed a mission to capture or kill Osama bin Laden in Abbottabad, Pakistan. Though ultimately successful, the intelligence leading up to the mission was riddled with uncertainty. There was no definitive confirmation that bin Laden was in the compound, and several critical assumptions were made under ambiguous circumstances. The SEALs had to rely heavily on their training, adaptability, and instincts to overcome unexpected developments during the mission.

This example illustrates a key truth: even successful operations can be compromised when intelligence is incomplete. The margin for error narrows, and the risk escalates. Leaders must factor in uncertainty and prepare contingencies accordingly.

Example 2: The Fallujah Offensive (2004) In 2004, U.S. forces launched a major operation in Fallujah, Iraq, based on intelligence indicating a stronghold of insurgents. However, once on the ground, the situation proved far more complex. Resistance was fiercer than anticipated, and the strategic assumptions underpinning the mission were quickly challenged. The operation suffered heavy casualties, and its objectives were only partially achieved.

This operation underscores how overreliance on flawed intelligence can lead to tactical missteps with devastating consequences. It highlights the critical need for intelligence that is not only accurate but also contextually grounded and continually updated.

Cultivating a Culture of Informed Decision-Making

To build a resilient and adaptive organization, leaders must cultivate a culture where informed decision-making is not an afterthought but a central pillar of the workplace ethos. This culture is shaped not only by access to quality data, but also by how people think, share, listen, and collaborate. It requires intentional effort to create an environment where diverse perspectives are sought, valued, and integrated into the decision-making process.

Below are key strategies that can guide leaders in developing this culture:

1. Foster Open Communication

Create an environment where team members feel safe and empowered to share their opinions—especially when those opinions challenge the status quo. Open communication doesn't just support collaboration; it fuels the exchange of ideas that can lead to transformative decisions.

Example: A tech startup might implement regular brainstorming sessions where team members are encouraged to pitch ideas without fear of criticism or dismissal. This kind of openness not only fosters innovation but reinforces the belief that every voice matters. By dismantling hierarchies of opinion, leaders can ensure that no valuable insight goes unheard—no matter how unorthodox it may seem at first.

2. Encourage Continuous Learning

A culture of informed decision-making is impossible without a parallel culture of learning. Leaders must not only promote but model intellectual curiosity—demonstrating that ongoing development is both encouraged and expected at every level of the organization.

Example: In the field of security, professionals routinely engage in continuous training to stay ahead of emerging threats. In the same way, organizations across all sectors should offer access to industry research, host internal knowledge-sharing sessions, and invest in skills development. By treating learning as a strategic asset, leaders prepare their teams to confront uncertainty with insight rather than instinct.

3. Utilize Data-Driven Insights

While intuition has its place, sustainable decision-making requires evidence. Leaders must harness the power of analytics to surface patterns, identify risks, and predict outcomes. But just as important as the data itself is how it's interpreted—through discussion, debate, and context-aware reasoning.

Example: A retail company analyzing regional sales data may notice that certain products perform better in specific locations. Rather than making decisions in isolation, the company invites regional managers to collaboratively assess the data. By weaving together statistical insight with on-the-ground knowledge, the business develops marketing strategies that are not only data-backed but locally relevant. This collaborative interpretation ensures that decisions are not just informed—but also deeply contextualized.

4. Emphasize Humility and Adaptability

Effective leadership begins with the recognition that no one person holds all the answers. Humility allows leaders to remain open to feedback, while adaptability enables them to revise decisions when better information becomes available. Together, these traits foster a dynamic rather than dogmatic decision-making culture.

Example: A leader might begin a team meeting by explicitly inviting alternative viewpoints and reinforcing the importance of shared decision-making. This can be complemented by publicly acknowledging when a team member's idea led to a breakthrough or averted a misstep. Such acts of humility model a growth mindset, encouraging team members to challenge assumptions and approach challenges as shared puzzles rather than top-down directives.

5. Celebrate Diverse Perspectives

Diversity in experience, background, and thought enriches the decision-making process, especially when those differences are recognized as strengths. Leaders must go beyond inclusion as a principle and actively elevate diverse viewpoints as integral to organizational success.

Example: During team retreats or strategic reviews, organizations might dedicate sessions to highlight how input from varied team members led to key decisions or innovations. These success stories don't just celebrate individuals—they reinforce a powerful message: collaboration across differences is a driver of excellence, not a compromise. When diversity is seen as a competitive advantage, it becomes woven into the organization's identity.

Conclusion: Cultivating a Culture of Informed Decision-Making

Informed decision-making is not simply the product of having access to information—it is the result of creating a culture where people are empowered to question, listen, and contribute. It requires courage to dissent, humility to change course, and discipline to continually seek out better understanding.

The analogy of the hub and spokes remains particularly resonant: the leader is the hub, connecting the diverse perspectives—the spokes—that give structure and strength to the whole. Just as a wheel cannot function with imbalanced or missing spokes, no decision can be complete without the integration of multiple viewpoints.

The more holistic the input, the more robust the output. A leader's role is not to have all the answers, but to ask the right questions, remain receptive to new ideas, and adapt when necessary. In doing so, they transform decision-making from a static act into a living, evolving process.

As these principles are practiced, the ripple effects are profound. Teams become more confident, more innovative, and more united. Collaboration becomes the default, not the exception. And the organization as a whole becomes not only more effective but more human—capable of navigating complexity with clarity, and change with grace.

Ultimately, cultivating a culture of informed decision-making is a long-term investment in people, potential, and purpose. It is the quiet force that shapes better outcomes and builds organizations that endure.

Chapter 12
Rule 10: "Earn trust and respect through demonstrating that you are true to yourself and to your word."

Integrity and Authenticity: The Foundation of True Leadership

Trust and respect are among the most crucial leadership qualities and without them, any leader can't influence or inspire. They are not given without effort or character but earned through actions, consistency, and character. Rule 10, Earn trust and respect if it is true to yourself and your word, deals with these core values of leadership by being truthful and authentic. A leader's power, after all, does not reside in authority alone but in how reliably they embody their words.

When we think of leadership, we get distracted by the skills and techniques that make a leader: communication, decision-making, or visionary thinking. All these qualities are essential, but with no integrity, they become hollow. Without a foundation of truthfulness, even the most brilliant ideas fall short in execution because people follow not just words, but values made visible through behavior. Integrity means consistency, staying true to your values, and being real in every circumstance. Authenticity, in turn, is critical to building relationships with your team and stakeholders. It gives weight to your words and credibility to your presence. A trustworthy and authentic leader builds deep-rooted loyalty and respect, both of which are indispensable for any leadership journey.

The idea behind this rule is that people follow what they believe in, not necessarily the person with the best credentials or résumé. It is not the list of achievements that draws loyalty, but the moral alignment and human connection. Leaders who are authentic build relationships that are built on honesty and openness. People want to work with and follow transparent leaders who make mistakes and do not try to cover their weaknesses or vulnerabilities. In fact, vulnerability, when coupled with accountability, can make leadership appear more courageous. The more real a leader is, the more people will believe in and respect him or her.

Why Integrity and Authenticity are Important in Leadership

Leaders with integrity are those who stand by their principles regardless of the circumstances. This does not mean following rules rigidly without flexibility or denying the value of other people's opinions. Instead, it means a leader's actions, choices, and language reflect his or her core values. These values are not seasonal; they are the throughline across difficult decisions and easy ones alike. You lead with integrity so your followers know what they should expect from you, and that predictability creates trust. People believe leaders who mean what they say and act accordingly. This predictability is the foundation of excellent relationships within a team, a company, or an organization. Consistency in principle gives clarity in uncertainty.

Being authentic does not necessarily mean being perfect. In fact, authentic leaders are generally the ones who are okay with being imperfect. They admit their faults, admit when they do not know something, and are responsible for their actions. They do not shield themselves behind the armor of authority; instead, they allow people to see their humanity. This particular vulnerability actually strengthens others' trust in them. Human leaders tend to win loyalty because people feel they can relate to them more personally, and their leadership seems more real and attainable. Authentic leadership means being yourself consistently with no external pressures or expectations as your true self. It is a leadership style that does not require performance but presence.

True leadership is realizing that your values drive your choices, words, and actions. These values become your compass for your decisions, small or big. In the face of moral dilemmas, value-driven leaders do not waver; they lean into their convictions even when it costs them ease or popularity. Your actions should reflect your values, not only consistency in your leadership style, but clarity for your followers, too. People respect leaders who know their principles and live by them, regardless of the tough situation. In times of crisis or ambiguity, this clarity becomes a lighthouse that others instinctively follow.

Building Trust by Being True to Your Word

The second half of Rule 10 is about keeping your word. Leaders who say they will do something and then do it increase their credibility. This is among the simplest ways to gain trust. It is a form of silent communication, a consistent message that "my word is enough." When leaders say they will do it, they must do it regardless of what it takes. When leaders break small promises, they risk losing trust and credibility. Even minor inconsistencies can erode confidence more deeply than one major failure.

Keeping promises, both small and big, has a cumulative effect. Each promise builds on the leader-follower bond over time. Over weeks and months, this creates a psychological contract far stronger than any formal agreement. Conversely, not delivering on promises can destroy trust and compromise a leader's character. This is true for significant strategic decisions and everyday interactions. For instance, a leader who tells their team they should check in on an issue or complete a task should do that. A promise of any size extends a leader's integrity, and its inability to fulfill it says a lot about the leader. Promises are not just obligations; instead, they are opportunities to show consistency in values and accountability.

But just how do you always keep your word? The first step would be being realistic about what you can and cannot afford. A commitment made in haste is often broken in regret. When leaders take on a lot or too much, they risk disappointing others when they fail. It is better to underpromise and overdeliver compared to the reverse.

Leaders who state their limits and make promises they believe they can keep tend to be more likely to maintain credibility and trustworthiness. Setting clear boundaries isn't a weakness, it's a strategic strength.

It is also important to remember that trust is built through consistency, not only through words. A leader who is inconsistent or frequently reneges on their word will not build relationships. They might earn compliance, but never true commitment. Trust grows in which expectations are regularly met; consistency is the key to that environment. Consistency reassures others that what you said yesterday will still be true tomorrow, and that kind of trust is difficult to break.

The Ripple Effect of Integrity in Leadership

The consequences of a leader being truthful and authentic go beyond the leader himself. Leadership, by its nature, is not confined to the individual; it ripples outward through teams, departments, and even entire cultures. Leaders define the culture of an organization. When leaders show integrity and authenticity, others follow suit. That creates a culture of honesty, accountability, and respect where people are at ease being themselves, which is crucial for high performance. People perform better when they don't have to wear a mask. Employees or followers trust their leaders more than they trust one another, which produces a collaborative, respectful, and open environment. In such spaces, creativity flourishes because fear diminishes.

This particular ripple effect is most apparent in teams. A leader who is trustworthy, true to their word, and true to themselves sets an excellent example for team members. Over time, this might develop a culture where teammates feel accountable to one another, knowing their words and actions matter as much as their leader's. Peer accountability becomes not a matter of pressure but of pride. They're more comfortable contributing ideas, taking risks, and being vulnerable, knowing they won't be judged or dismissed. This can make innovation and growth possible and even encouraged. Psychological safety becomes the fertile ground in which bold thinking can thrive.

Authenticity is also essential for a leader to communicate effectively. Authentic leaders communicate more naturally, and their followers will relate to them less easily. There is no pretense to cut through, just a person speaking to another person. Authentic communication builds trust because people know when a leader is sincere. We are more attuned to tone than we often realize; sincerity is sensed more than it is understood. Leaders who speak out of the heart and express their thoughts honestly create an environment where others can speak freely. This results in better collaboration, improved problem-solving, and much better results. In time, communication ceases to be a transactional exchange and becomes a channel for alignment, engagement, and shared purpose.

The Challenges of Maintaining Integrity and Authenticity

Integrity and authenticity are essential but not always easy to maintain, particularly in challenging situations. There will always be moments when leaders are urged to compromise or do something contrary to their beliefs. The business world, for instance, presents ethical quandaries that tempt leaders to scrimp or even to give in to short-term expediency. The pressure to achieve results, secure client satisfaction, or maintain a competitive edge can push leaders toward decisions that feel pragmatic in the moment but come at the cost of principle. The real test of leadership is when a leader is quizzed about their integrity and authenticity.

Maintaining integrity also entails the ability to make tough decisions. Doing what is right is often not the simplest choice and might involve risks. Sometimes, the consequences of standing firm in your values may include financial setbacks, strained relationships, or professional isolation. But the long-term rewards of sticking to your values outweigh the pain of hard decisions. Over time, integrity compounds like interest, it builds a reputation, creates credibility, and invites deeper loyalty. People who choose the right path, even the tough path, get followers' respect and develop long, long-lasting relationships. Such relationships are based on respect and trust and are the foundation of any leadership journey. These bonds serve as the unseen scaffolding that holds organizations and movements together.

Yet another barrier to authenticity is conformity to social or organizational norms. Leaders, especially those at the top, might need to project a version of themselves that is consistent with industry or organizational standards or expectations. They often feel obligated to perform roles scripted by culture, position, or stakeholder demands. But this kind of 'masking' can result in burnout, frustration, and a lack of fulfillment. When leaders regularly edit themselves to fit a mold, they eventually lose sight of their core identity. If leaders think they must pretend to be something they cannot be, they cannot build relationships with others, and their leadership is less effective. Authenticity loses its power when it's watered down by the fear of not fitting in.

Stay grounded in your values to conquer these challenges. Remember why you're a leader and who you are as a leader. Let your purpose be your anchor when circumstances try to sway you. This self-awareness will help you keep your word, no matter if pressure is mounting. You should also have a network of colleagues, supporters, and mentors who can keep you true to your values. These allies serve as your sounding boards, your mirrors, and your reminders of the leader you set out to be.

The Impact of Trust and Respect on Long-Term Leadership Success

Leaders who prioritize trust and respect and demonstrate integrity and authenticity are the ones who create sustainable success. They plant seeds that bloom over time, shaping not just outcomes but cultures. Once you earn their trust and respect, you develop a foundation for your leadership, staff, company, and yourself. This foundation is strong enough to withstand disruption, failure, and uncertainty. Trust and respect work as a feedback loop; people who trust and respect you are much more likely to back you, and vice versa, as a leader.

Trust and respect have far-reaching, long-term benefits. People trust you much more; they will go above and beyond, do their best work, and stay with you through difficult times. In the long run, people won't remember your title or your metrics; they'll remember how you made them feel—valued, safe, and believed in. You will be viewed as somebody who leads for the common good, and they will follow you. Such leaders become moral compasses, not just managers.

Ultimately, leadership is all about relationships, motivating others, and developing a culture of respect and trust. Rule 10 reminds us to earn trust and respect by being true to ourselves, our word, and our values. This authenticity leads others to follow, making a leader a legacy that lasts well beyond their time in office. Legacies aren't built through charisma or cleverness, but through constancy in character.

The Bonds of Trust and Respect: Stories from the Trenches

Okay, let's get real with some stories. Sometimes, the best way to understand something is to see it done, to know about the moments that mattered and made a difference. Leadership lessons aren't always born in boardrooms—they are lived in mud, sweat, silence, and decision.

The Rugby Brotherhood

For me, rugby was more than a game. It was a battlefield where trust and respect were earned in the heat of battle, friendships were constructed in sweat and mud, and camaraderie went beyond the score. The pitch didn't just test skill—it tested heart.

One game stands out to me in particular. It was a week's local derby against arch-rivals. The atmosphere was electric, the stands had been packed, and the stakes had been higher. We knew going onto the field this was more than a game—a character test, a fight of pride—a demonstration of who the team was.

It was a brutal match from the beginning. The tackles were heavy, the weather conditions were severe, and the tempo was fast. We were down a few points with minutes remaining, and it was on our shoulders. But the scoreboard wasn't the only thing to matter in those final minutes. It was about being there for one another, having one another's backs, and showing we were going to fight to the end whistle.

Then, something happened in the final minutes. We dug deep, and with willpower, we began playing with a type of synchronicity formed over years of shared pain and persistence. We helped, covered each other's weaknesses, and celebrated each other's strengths.

I remember making a crucial pass to a teammate struggling all match. It was a split-second decision to trust him to catch that ball and make that run. He did, and it paid off with the try, which got us the game.

There was no individual glory explosion when we crossed the try line. No one stood out in particular. What was important was that we fought together and each of us played our part. We'd won that victory simply because we trusted and respected one another.

That experience and countless others on the rugby pitch taught me about teamwork. It showed me how much more you can do when you value and trust one another, not only in your own ability but in your teammates' capability. That game made me realize trust and respect aren't abstract ideals—they are lived behaviors, forged and proven under fire.

The Bodyguard's Code

Trust and respect were more than abstract concepts to me as a bodyguard: they were daily life-and-death concerns. You don't just talk about trust, you breathe it, wear it, and bet your life on it. Trust and respect become the basis of your relationship when you're responsible for another person's safety and placing your personal life in danger to protect theirs.

One assignment actually sticks with me. I was protecting an extremely high-profile CEO going to an extremely volatile region. Security worries were great, and the risks were real. In those moments, trust becomes less about words and more about intuition and intention.

I remember meeting this CEO for the first time—a successful businessman, a man used to controlling his daily life. But he lost his composure when we talked about the threats. He knew he could not go through this by himself. But what struck me was how much he trusted me—somebody who was a stranger to him then.

We talked all night, and he said he was worried about the threats in addition to himself. And he trusted me with much more than his physical safety, he trusted me with his psychological safety. I knew then how much responsibility I had. His trust was a heavy burden on me.

I had to act fast and make decisions under pressure on a few parts of the trip. We had to divert routes, adjust security, and make split-second calls about people we spoke to. However, more than anything, what I needed was his trust. And most of all, I had to show him I cared about him, that I was thinking about his best interests. That emotional contract, unspoken but deeply felt, was what kept us both safe.

That mission and numerous others in close protection taught me the value of trust and respect. It's not about having the skills or training. It's about the bonds you develop and your loyalty. These qualities transcend cultural differences, language barriers, and even life-threatening situations and create lasting bonds. Loyalty is earned not through obedience, but through mutual regard and shared risk.

The Business Battlefield

Trust and respect aren't life or death in the corporate world, but they matter in building teams, negotiating complex deals, and attaining common objectives. In business, reputation is the currency that matters most.

I remember one specific deal—a high-stakes merger with several parties with competing interests. The negotiations had been intense, and the pressure was incredible. There were moments when it appeared like the deal could snap at any moment because each side was refusing to budge, with each one clinging to their terms.

However, the deal did not collapse, and what truly sealed it was not the financial terms or the legal framework. It was trust. We had spent weeks establishing relationships with the other parties and being truthful about their concerns. We were negotiating the relationship along with the deal.

We'd shown ourselves fair and reliable. We never let the pressure determine who we were when times were tough. We listened, we communicated, and we made sure everybody felt respected. That trust, built over months, was the basis of the agreement. And that respect ensured the deal was done right and set the stage for future partnerships.

That experience reinforced the need for trust and respect in business. They're the lifeblood of collaborations—they aren't just formalities. These qualities turn possible conflicts into chances for growth and competitive environments into ones that benefit everybody. Trust transforms transactions into relationships, and respect transforms deals into legacies.

The Inner Battle

But the biggest battles have been with me—fights with self-doubt, fear, and the demons that whisper my insecurities into my ear. It would be very easy to dismiss such things as trivial, but anyone who has fought similar battles knows they are realistic. They are not metaphorical—they are lived, intimate confrontations that can drain your will and cloud your sense of purpose.

These inner struggles don't arrive with warning signs. They sneak in during the quiet moments, when the applause has faded, the pressure is mounting, or the loneliness of leadership becomes deafening. Doubt creeps in like a shadow, casting itself over even the strongest convictions, and fear magnifies the cracks we try so hard to hide. But these are the crucibles where real leaders are forged—not in moments of applause, but in the silence of personal reckoning.

In times of vulnerability, the trust and respect I've gotten from people like my family, friends, and colleagues have given me the courage to go through those things and emerge much stronger than before. They became my anchor points, like steady hands on my back when my own knees buckled under the weight of expectation and responsibility.

There have been moments when I doubted if I could lead or overcome what was before me. But the belief others have in me—their faith in my abilities and values—has kept me going. Sometimes, we borrow strength from the people who believe in us, even when our own reservoir runs dry. Those people stood with me and reminded me of who I am and who trusted me when I did not trust myself. They saw light in me when I was fumbling in the dark.

When we are most vulnerable and insecure, the trust and respect others give us often keep us moving. Those are the times when we discover we're not alone. People we trust, have faith in, and respect are our pillars whenever we feel like falling. Their presence becomes our compass when the road ahead blurs, and their confidence becomes the mirror that reflects our better selves back to us.

The Tapestry of Trust and Respect

These stories and numerous others from my life have produced a thread of trust and respect in my leadership style and interactions with others. Over time, they've woven themselves into a larger tapestry, a rich, complex design of moments, decisions, relationships, and lessons. They have shown me that trust and respect aren't abstract concepts but the foundation of relationships. They are not items to be checked off on a leadership checklist; they are living principles that must be practiced, nurtured, and protected.

They are the glue that holds teams together, the fuel that inspires collaboration, and the foundation of any endeavor. In every arena, whether high-stakes or day-to-day, they quietly shape outcomes by empowering people to bring their best selves forward. They make it safe to speak up, to challenge ideas respectfully, to admit mistakes, and to share credit. Without trust and respect, even the most brilliant strategies fall flat because people aren't invested in each other or the mission.

Trust and respect are important for good leadership. They are the foundation for establishing great teams, overcoming problems, and attaining amazing achievements. True leaders are those who create loyalty and cultivate these qualities. And they do so not with words alone, but with choices made in the margins when nobody's watching, when the pressure is high, and when standing firm is harder than giving in.

Through these experiences, I have discovered that trust and respect come from actions, not words. They're shown in the rough times, the sacrifices we make for other people, the respect we display, and the honesty we possess. They're carved into the fiber of our leadership by the quiet consistency of character and the deliberate honoring of others' dignity.

In every field, whether on the rugby pitch, as a bodyguard, in business, or in the fight within, these qualities remain the cornerstones of success. They are the common thread that binds victories and failures, silence and speech, resilience and vulnerability.

As I move along this journey, respect and trust will always be there for me personally to push me forward, to lead with conviction. Because trust and respect are, in the end, much more than values; they're a legacy. Not a legacy written in stone or medals, but etched in the hearts and memories of those we've impacted. They are the invisible bridges we build between ourselves and others—bridges that, if built with care, will outlast our titles, our achievements, and even our time.

Building Bridges of Trust: Practical Advice for Leaders

So, let's get right to building trust. We discussed its importance and saw real-world examples—now let's get rolling. However, trust does not come about by chance; you build it brick by brick with hard work, real connection, and determination to be the leader people want to follow. It's not earned with grand speeches or polished presentations but in the quiet, consistent choices made each day—the ones that speak volumes about who you are and what you stand for when no one's watching.

Think of trust as a bridge. It links people, allows open communication, and creates a space for collaboration and shared success. But a strong bridge requires work and materials. You wouldn't just chuck some planks over a chasm and hope for the best, right? No way! You'd design the framework with intention, choose the strongest materials, and hire skilled hands to bring the vision to life. Just like that, leadership requires careful, continuous effort, not just quick fixes or shortcuts.

But what makes trust buildable? What are the nuts and bolts, the beams and rivets, that make the bridge between you and your team and stakeholders strong enough to withstand pressure and time? How do you build that connection that enables long-term relationships and sustainable success?

1. Be Reliable and Consistent

Reliability is the bedrock on which you build a bridge of trust—be reliable and consistent. You earn a reputation for dependability and trustworthiness by keeping your promises, commitments, and actions. People know they can depend on you—that you'll do what you say you will do—when you say you will. And that predictability creates a feeling of security and peace of mind; people can relax knowing they're in good hands, free to focus their energy on the tasks at hand rather than second-guessing your word.

Just picture it this way: Imagine meeting a friend for coffee. They're not there for you when it matters if they show up late, cancel at the last minute, or "forget" their wallet again! That inconsistency may seem small, but it chips away at the foundation of the relationship, creating a subtle sense of doubt. However, being on time, following through on commitments, and showing up when you say you will makes you feel like you can trust them, and over time, that reliability becomes a bond that strengthens friendship.

Same with leadership. People expect you to be consistent—consistent not only in results but in tone, values, and treatment. When you act with uniformity in your decisions, keep your principles intact even when challenged, and remain steady during crises, you show your team that you are someone they can count on, not just in calm but especially in chaos. They know you will not flip-flop on your decisions, play favourites, or throw them under the bus when things get tough. This consistency gives your team the stability and psychological safety they need to take risks, perform confidently, and bring their full selves to the table.

2. Communicate Openly and Honestly

Communication is the mortar between the bricks of trust—open and honest dialogue binds people together and strengthens the structure. You build trust and understanding by communicating openly, sharing information freely, and listening to your team and stakeholders. You knock down those walls of secrecy and suspicion and create room for open dialogue, constructive feedback, and a common goal. Clarity replaces confusion, and confidence replaces hesitation.

Just picture it this way: Imagine building a house with contractors. If everybody works off different blueprints, does not communicate their plans, and keeps secrets from each other, the house will be a disaster. The walls will be wrong, the plumbing won't connect, and the roof might cave in! Each person's well-intended actions won't add up to a coherent whole without a shared vision and open communication. Misalignment leads to missteps, and the cost is often more than just money—it's trust, time, and morale.

But if everyone communicates openly, shares their ideas, and works toward a common vision, the house will be a masterpiece of collaboration and cooperation. Misunderstandings are addressed early, creative ideas are welcomed, and everyone feels like they are a vital part of something larger than themselves.

Similarly, in leadership, open communication with your team—combined with transparency in intent and clarity in delivery—creates a culture of trust that permeates every level of the organization. When information isn't hoarded but shared, when feedback flows in both directions, and when listening becomes just as important as speaking, people begin to feel like more than employees—they feel like trusted contributors. Participants feel valued, respected, and involved in decision-making. They're not just told what to do—they're brought into the *why*, and that inclusion fuels ownership, loyalty, and innovation. Employees are more inclined to support your vision, rally behind tough calls, and give their best when they feel part of a team—not just a cog in a machine.

3. Show Respect and Appreciation

Respect and appreciation are like the decorative touches that make a bridge not only functional but beautiful—elements that, while subtle, transform cold structure into something meaningful. You create a trusting environment if you show respect to your team and stakeholders and acknowledge their efforts with genuine appreciation. It's like the finishing touches on a house—polished woodwork, warm lighting, and cozy details—that make it feel like a home, a space where people feel welcome, safe, and valued.

Just picture it this way: imagine having a dinner party with your friends. You won't make your guests feel valued if you ignore them, criticize their attire, or serve them burnt food with indifference. But when you greet them warmly at the door, engage in meaningful conversation, and serve them a thoughtfully prepared meal—even if imperfect—it sends a message: "You matter. You're worth the effort." That's how friendship is strengthened—through small, sincere acts of care and recognition.

Same with leadership. You create an environment where people feel seen, respected, and motivated by consistently demonstrating respect to your team members—listening to their input, valuing their time, and acknowledging their efforts publicly and privately. This builds loyalty and commitment and motivates people to give their best work not out of obligation, but from a place of genuine investment and connection. Respect fuels resilience; appreciation fuels growth.

4. Embrace Vulnerability

Recognizing vulnerability may seem counterintuitive to building trust—especially in high-stakes environments—but vulnerability is a powerful way to build real, lasting relationships. When you show your human side and admit your mistakes and struggles, you create an environment of authenticity and empathy that builds trust and fosters psychological safety. It's like showing your team that you're not some untouchable superhero leader who's always right and never fazed—but rather a real person navigating the same storm, learning as you go, and doing your best to lead with heart.

Just picture it this way: imagine meeting someone new. If they appear perfect—flawless in speech, posture, and confidence—they may impress you but are likely difficult to relate to. However, if they reveal their struggles, their anxieties, or moments where they fell and got back up, you'll probably feel a stronger connection. You'll see them not as someone above you, but beside you—a peer in the human experience. And that's where real trust is born.

Same with leadership. You build trust when you're willing to share your vulnerabilities with your team, admit your mistakes without defensiveness, and share your struggles without shame. You come across to them as a real person—someone they can relate to, someone they can talk to, someone unafraid of being human. This creates a deeper, more resilient connection, and in turn, your team becomes more open, more supportive, and more willing to bring their full, imperfect selves to the table—which is exactly what a healthy, high-functioning culture needs.

5. Empower and Delegate

Delegating duties and empowering your team demonstrates your commitment to their growth, your trust in their potential, and your belief in their abilities. It is the leadership equivalent of saying, *"I trust you to carry this,"* and more importantly, *"I see greatness in you, and I'm not afraid to let it rise."* This promotes ownership and accountability and fosters a more engaged, autonomous, and motivated team.

Just picture it this way: imagine yourself as a sports team coach. If you micromanage every play, shout instructions constantly, and criticize every mistake, you won't make your players feel trusted or empowered. Instead, they'll second-guess themselves, shrink under pressure, and hesitate to take initiative. But if you let them make their own plays, support their decisions, and encourage thoughtful risk-taking—even when it doesn't always work out—you'll cultivate players who grow in skill, confidence, and unity. They'll rise not in fear, but in ownership.

That's also true for leadership in the workplace. When you delegate responsibility, trust your team with meaningful tasks, and give them the freedom to make decisions, you're not just lightening your own load—you're actively building their leadership muscles. You show them their voice matters, their work is essential, and that they are not just helpers but contributors to the mission. This creates a workplace where people don't wait to be told what to do—they anticipate, innovate, and take action with pride.

6. Be Consistent in Your Actions and Values

Consistency is the cornerstone of trust. When people know they can rely on your words aligning with your actions and your actions aligning with your values, you establish a clear, dependable rhythm in your leadership. Without consistency, even well-meaning leaders appear unpredictable or insincere. It's like building a house with one set of blueprints but constructing it using another entirely—the result is chaos, and no one wants to live in a house that feels like it might collapse at any moment.

Just picture it this way: imagine following a recipe for a cake. If you randomly substitute ingredients, skip steps, or bake it at the wrong temperature, the end result is likely a disaster. One bite in, and you know something's off—even if it looks fine on the outside. But when you follow the recipe with intention, measure carefully, and remain consistent throughout the process, the cake becomes not only delicious but dependable—a testament to your discipline and care.

Same with leadership. People expect you to walk your talk. When you act consistently in your decisions, language, and treatment of others, people stop bracing for surprises or contradictions. They know you won't play favorites, bend the rules, or flip on your convictions when pressure mounts. This kind of consistency breeds psychological safety—it allows your team to operate with confidence, make bold moves, and trust that your leadership will remain steady no matter how turbulent the winds get. It's not about being rigid—it's about being reliable, which, in the long run, earns far more respect than any momentary brilliance.

7. Seek and Offer Feedback

Feedback helps you build and maintain trust. It's a two-way street—constant communication that helps you understand your team's perspective, address their concerns, and move them toward improvement. Actively solicit feedback from your team and stakeholders—and be willing to give constructive criticism when necessary. It's an expression of your open communication, your commitment to continuous improvement, and a shared investment in mutual growth.

Just picture it this way: imagine you're learning a new dance move. If you refuse to take your instructor's feedback, ignore their corrections, and stubbornly keep making the same mistakes, you're not getting better. You'll be stuck, frustrated, and eventually settle for mediocrity. But if you approach them with humility, ask for feedback, and adjust based on their advice—even if it stings a little—you start to unlock potential. The move becomes smoother, more confident, and soon enough, second nature.

Same with leadership. By actively seeking feedback from your team, you send a clear message: *"Your perspective matters, and I'm not above learning from you."* You show them that leadership isn't a fixed position—it's a dynamic process rooted in growth. At the same time, offering thoughtful, respectful, and actionable feedback creates clarity and direction. People can only improve when they understand where they stand and how to move forward. Over time, this open exchange cultivates a culture where vulnerability isn't feared—it's welcomed as the starting point of excellence. Trust is no longer fragile or situational—it becomes a foundation of shared progress where everyone rises together.

8. Celebrate Successes and Acknowledge Mistakes

Celebrating successes and acknowledging mistakes builds trust and accountability. You celebrate achievements because you appreciate what your people did—it could be a pat on the back, a spontaneous high-five, a shout-out in a meeting, or even a standing ovation for a job well done. Recognition isn't just about rewards—it's a message that says *"I see you. Your work matters."* On the flip side, admitting mistakes demonstrates humility, a willingness to grow, and the courage to lead with honesty. It's like saying, *"Yes, we all stumble—but how we respond is what sets us apart."*

Just picture it this way: imagine you're a parent raising a child. If you only criticize their mistakes and never praise their efforts or celebrate their wins, they'll begin to question their worth. Over time, they may become discouraged, lose motivation, and stop trying altogether. But if you celebrate their successes, applaud their progress, and help them reflect on their missteps without shame, they'll grow in confidence. They'll learn not to fear failure but to see it as part of the journey—a stepping stone, not a stop sign.

That's also true in leadership. When you take the time to celebrate your team's accomplishments, no matter how big or small, it reaffirms their value. It creates momentum and morale—a sense that the effort was seen, the late nights were worth it, and that what they do contributes to something larger. At the same time, when leaders are willing to acknowledge their own mistakes—and create space for others to do the same—it nurtures psychological safety. Teams begin to take smarter risks, speak up more freely, and collaborate more openly because they know that failure won't be punished but used as a platform for growth. This honest acknowledgment of both victory and vulnerability fosters a culture of mutual accountability, trust, and continual evolution—where progress is celebrated and learning never ends.

Chapter 13
Conclusion

As we arrive at a close, the following are some lessons and principles learned along the way. Like ten solid pillars supporting an enormous structure, these rules can help you create a lasting legacy of leadership. They are not mere suggestions but timeless truths that, when practiced with intention, serve as the architecture of trust, influence, and meaningful progress.

1. Embrace the Power of "Yes":

Develop a proactive and positive attitude, seize opportunities, and face challenges with a can-do attitude. Saying "yes" allows for brand-new experiences, collaboration, and potential. Remember that every "yes" is a chance to learn, develop, and expand. And while not every opportunity may be comfortable or easy, the very act of leaning into the unknown can unlock paths that were once unimaginable. Leaders who say "yes" with discernment are often those who discover the full stretch of their capabilities—and inspire others to do the same.

2. Take Initiative and Be Accountable:

Don't wait for permission—get involved and be responsible for your actions. Use your judgement, make decisions confidently, and learn from your mistakes. Initiative paired with accountability enables you to act with courage and integrity to move forward and motivate others. It also builds your credibility over time, as people begin to trust not only your words but the weight of your actions. Leaders are not only judged by what they start, but also by what they're willing to own—especially when things don't go as planned.

3. Embrace Problem-Solving:

See challenges as opportunities for innovation and growth. Believe that all problems have a solution—even if it costs money. Be resourceful, creative, and persistent when searching for solutions that help your team and organization. Remember that finding a solution may cost money, emotional or even personal, but it takes leadership to find solutions. True problem-solvers do not merely fix what is broken—they anticipate obstacles, frame failure as feedback, and rally others toward possibilities that did not exist before the problem appeared.

4. Take Ownership, Not Just Notice:

Point out issues, but own them. Be the person who says, "I got this!" Avoid the "imaginary someone," and develop a culture of accountability in which everyone is responsible for their actions and solutions. Ownership means more than just raising a flag when something's wrong—it means rolling up your sleeves to be part of the solution, even when it wasn't your mess to begin with. That shift from passive observer to active contributor is what separates the average from the impactful.

5. Learn from Mistakes:

Accept a growth mindset—mistakes are unavoidable, but learning opportunities exist. Analyze your errors, discover exactly where you can improve, and learn from them to improve and avoid future mistakes. Remember, "Anyone can make a mistake. Twice is stupidity. Three times is incompetence; there'll be no fourth time." Each mistake, when approached with honesty and self-reflection, becomes a data point on your leadership journey. The true failure isn't in falling short—it's in refusing to examine why and how to rise smarter the next time.

6. Find Your Passion and Purpose:

Do what you care about and care about what you do. Find fulfillment in your personal values by merging them with your professional goals. Passion and purpose are the ingredients for motivation, resilience, and innovation in leadership. They are the internal engines that keep leaders moving forward when external recognition fades. When purpose fuels your vision and passion animates your work, people don't just follow your title—they follow your fire.

7. Value Diverse Perspectives:

Encourage respectful dissent, acknowledging that everybody has the right to speak out. Accept constructive criticism and open communication to question assumptions, lessen bias, and build better solutions. Diversity in thought, background, and experience is not a box to be checked—it's a strategic advantage. Great leaders not only tolerate opposing views; they welcome them as catalysts for clarity, creativity, and growth. It's in the friction of different perspectives that the spark of innovation most often ignites.

8. Embrace Feedback:

Consider negative or positive feedback as a gift—a tool for development and growth. Ask for feedback, listen without judgement, and use it to enhance and become a much better leader. Remember, "Learning how to do something wrong means being told you did it wrong." Feedback, when genuinely sought and humbly received, acts as a mirror—reflecting both your blind spots and your brilliance. Leaders who are open to being shaped are the ones who eventually shape the world around them.

9. Practice Empathy and Understanding:

Recognize everybody sees the world differently. Try to understand their viewpoints, experiences, and motivations. Actively listen, ask tough questions, and find common ground to bridge understanding gaps and encourage collaboration. Empathy is not about agreeing—it's about acknowledging. It transforms command into connection, and strategy into service. In a world fractured by division, leaders who empathize do more than lead—they heal, unite, and build lasting allegiance rooted in shared humanity.

10. Lead with Integrity and Authenticity:

Be true to yourself, your values, and your word. Earn trust and respect through consistency, transparency, and accountability. Lead by example—produce a culture of authenticity and integrity. These traits don't just guide behavior—they define legacy. People may forget your titles and your tactics, but they will never forget how your honesty made them feel safe, or how your authenticity gave them permission to lead from the truth of who they are.

Your Leadership Journey Begins Here

Now you are done reading through this book and are prepared to take your own leadership journey, take these ten principles and make them yours. They aren't rules you must adhere to, but a compass you should utilize as a place to start—a framework you can alter to fit your circumstances and ambitions. Let them evolve with you as you grow, and revisit them often as you face new challenges, questions, and opportunities.

Remember that leadership is a journey of development, discovery, and learning. It is about taking risks, learning from mistakes, and constantly attempting to improve yourself—not for perfection, but for purpose. Great leadership is not born overnight; it is sculpted by time, shaped by failure, and refined by every small decision to lead with intention.

Here are a few thoughts to guide you as you embark on this exciting adventure:

1. Embrace Your Unique Style

There's no one-size-fits-all approach to leadership. Our experiences, weaknesses, and strengths influence our leadership style. Accept your own uniqueness, your quirks, and your real self. Don't attempt to be somebody you're not—be the very best version of yourself. Let your authenticity shine through in how you speak, how you lead, and how you connect with others. People follow leaders who are real, not rehearsed.

Picture this: In a world where everything was the same color, where flowers looked identical, birds sang the same song, and all trees stood in perfect symmetry—what a dull, uninspiring world that would be. Diversity is what makes nature vibrant, and it's what makes leadership powerful. Your voice, your story, your lived experiences—these are not obstacles to overcome but assets to harness. Embrace your style, your scars, and your strengths; that's what makes you not just a leader, but a remarkable one.

2. Be Bold, Be Courageous

Leadership requires courage. Courage to make challenging choices, question the status quo, and stand for what you believe. Do not fear taking chances, moving beyond your comfort zone, and taking on new challenges. Leadership is rarely convenient or safe—it demands boldness even when the outcome is uncertain.

Imagine an explorer entering uncharted territory. They do not know what lies ahead, but they are driven by the spirit of adventure, the hunger for discovery, and the willingness to risk failure in search of something greater. Leadership is like that exploration—it asks you to forge paths where none existed, to walk alone before others can follow, and to navigate ambiguity with grace and grit. The road less traveled may be daunting, but it's often the one that leads to true transformation.

3. Build Bridges—Not Walls

Leadership isn't for the solo person. It's about relationships, collaboration, and community building. Connect with your team, co-workers, and stakeholders. Listen to them, understand their needs, and work together towards common goals. Leadership is not about being in charge—it's about being in service to something greater than yourself.

Think it over this way: Suppose a world without bridges. We'd all be alone on our little islands, unable to communicate with one another, share thoughts, or create anything meaningful together. Bridges connect—they span the distance between difference and understanding. They carry the weight of people's hopes, fears, and potential. As a leader, your job is to be the architect of those bridges. Build spaces where others feel heard, included, and supported. When you lead with connection, you don't just build a team—you create a movement.

4. Embrace the Power of "And"

Fear not the power of "and." Rather than settling for either/or thinking or choosing between seemingly competing priorities, look for ways to blend ideas and craft solutions that serve multiple goals at once. True leadership lies not in division, but in synthesis—in recognizing that creativity often lives in the space between polarities.

Imagine this: If you had to choose only vanilla or chocolate, coffee or tea, night or day, life would quickly become monochrome. "And" allows for flavor, for balance, for complexity. It makes room for innovation, not just compromise. The same principle applies to leadership. When you embrace "and," you invite flexibility, unity, and possibility. It enables you to gather diverse perspectives, harmonize opposing views, and unlock holistic, multi-dimensional solutions.

5. Never Stop Learning

The world is in constant motion, and so are the demands of leadership. That's why the best leaders never stop learning. They stay curious, hungry, and humble—recognizing that each moment is a chance to grow, unlearn, and stretch beyond the familiar. Leadership isn't about having all the answers; it's about constantly seeking better ones.

Think about it this way: a shark must keep swimming or it sinks. For leaders, learning is the motion that keeps us agile, afloat, and alive in the turbulent currents of change. Whether you're reading, listening, reflecting, or experimenting, the commitment to lifelong learning is what transforms leadership from a role into a practice. Growth doesn't happen in hindsight—it lives in the now, in your willingness to evolve before you're forced to.

6. Celebrate the Journey

Leadership is not just about arriving at destinations—it's about walking the road with joy, gratitude, and reflection. Celebrate the wins, even the small ones. Honor your team, acknowledge their effort, and find meaning in the stumbles as well as the strides.

Imagine climbing a mountain. It's not just about reaching the summit—it's about the sunrise you catch at base camp, the stories shared over campfires, and the breathless moments where the view takes your words away. Leadership mirrors that climb. It tests you, shapes you, surprises you. And if you wait until the very top to celebrate, you'll miss the wonder of the ascent. So pause. Look around. Celebrate what's working. Thank the people beside you. Enjoy the climb.

7. Make a Difference

Ultimately, leadership is not about power—it's about impact. It's about using your influence, your voice, and your presence to create change that outlasts you. Make a difference in the lives of your team, your organization, and your community. Do good not for applause, but for legacy.

Imagine a world where each person decided to use their strengths to lift others, to solve problems, to improve systems. What a world of innovation, inclusion, and kindness that would be. Leadership gives you a chance to be part of that vision—not just by leading with ambition, but by leading with heart. When you align your actions with a cause greater than yourself, you don't just manage people—you inspire them.

Remember these words as you take your leadership journey forward: be courageous in moments of doubt, be real in a world that often rewards masks, be brave enough to lead where others won't, and be kind enough to never forget the humanity behind every goal. Be the leader the world doesn't just admire—but the one it needs.

Your journey begins now. Step forward not with certainty, but with purpose. Not with perfection, but with integrity. And as you go, may the lessons you've learned here become not just thoughts you remember, but principles you live by.

Go Forth and Lead with Courage

Remember, leadership is not a title, a position, or a fixed set of skills—it is a journey, a mindset, and a daily commitment to service, growth, and integrity. It is the quiet resolve to face challenges head-on, the humility to admit mistakes, and the relentless drive to become better—not just for yourself, but for those who look to you for guidance.

Leadership is the courage to take ownership in uncertain times, to stand firmly in your truth, and to lead with authenticity even when the path is unclear. It is the capacity to foster trust, to cultivate collaboration, and to create spaces where every voice matters and every person is empowered to bring their full selves to the table.

It is about discovering your passion, aligning your values with your vision, and pursuing a mission that resonates with your soul. It is about leaving a mark—not for recognition, but for impact. It is about making a difference, lifting others as you rise, and inspiring the same in those you lead.

The path of leadership is rarely smooth. There will be setbacks, failures, and moments of self-doubt. But it is in these crucibles of uncertainty that true leadership reveals itself. When you face adversity with grace, respond to mistakes with humility, and rise again with newfound wisdom—that is when you become the leader you were meant to be.

Remember the ten rules we've explored throughout this book. They are not mere suggestions, but enduring principles forged through lived experience, reflection, and resilience. Let them serve as your compass. Adapt them to your style, your values, your context—and let them evolve as you do.

Embrace the power of "yes." Take initiative, hold yourself accountable, and remain a student of life. Find your purpose and lead from it. Build trust through action, communicate with honesty, and listen with empathy. Value diverse perspectives, seek feedback with humility, and never stop growing.

Leadership is not about being in charge—it is about being in service. It is about leaving the world a little kinder, more just, and more hopeful than you found it.

Your leadership is needed now more than ever. The world is waiting for people with vision, compassion, and the resolve to drive meaningful change. Step forward. Take risks. Raise your voice. This future is not something that will simply arrive—it's something we must build, together.

So go forth—with courage, with clarity, and with an unshakable commitment to your calling. Meet the challenges head-on. Learn from them. Lift others as you climb. Lead in a way that invites others to lead too.

Believe in yourself. Believe in your team. Believe in the power of leadership to change lives, to heal wounds, and to build a better tomorrow for all.

The road ahead may be uncertain, but the purpose is clear—and the destination is worth every step. Lead with courage. Lead with heart. And above all, lead in a way that leaves a legacy.

The world is waiting.

Go make it happen.

Made in the USA
Columbia, SC
28 July 2025

61023130R00122